James P Gavin.

I am a retired lorry driver for almost half a century driving around the country delivering anything and everything, from coffee to coffins.
I have never actually delivered any babies, but one time came close to doing just that. But that is another story.
My driving ambition now is to deliver to you my attempts at story telling.
They say that there is a story in everyone, of that I have no doubt. But how to deliver that story? Well, my friend's life is one long road of learning, and that road I took late in my life. But I am prepared to give it my best shot.
Storytelling is in my blood; it has been in my paternal family since...
Well since forever.
 I listened intently as a child and watched closely as the storytellers used facial expressions, hand movements, and verbally accentuated to help animate the story.
So, through the skill of the storyteller, my mind pictured the many different heroes that I could visualize with ease.
I could almost touch, taste, and smell, the action.
A hard act to follow.
But I am here to try and emulate my forefathers.

    I hope that you enjoy this story.

Hogan's Hell
(The power of the mind)

Jimmy Hogan was in his local Doctors surgery, in Luton, glancing through a national newspaper in the crowded waiting room.

The only reason for him being at the doctor's was for a mild skin disorder some sort of rash that he picked up at one place or another.

An unwanted disease left graciously by some unwashed creature who had an aversion to soap and water, of which there were many in this modern day of newly evolved Viruses.

He sat there reading the paper without absorbing anything; he was just going through the motions to avoid looking at or talking to any of the other patients.

There was another reason why he disliked reading newspapers? That was because it was old, heard before news, second-hand news, yesterday's televised news.

He flicked through the paper, slowly making his way towards the crossword puzzle. Then something caught his eye.

The story was about a family who were claiming that their house was haunted and that they had been physically attacked by all sorts of ghosts and demons and were unable to live in the house.

Hogan Laughed out loud then remembered where he

was, he read more into the story and again started laughing out loud, caring not who heard him.
'Absolute fucking morons, these Pratts will do anything to get their picture in the papers' he said aloud.
He started laughing yet again, and the people close to him moved away, he glanced at them and shrugged, he was used to it.
Hogan was a sceptic in the full sense of the word, he would tell anyone willing to listen That there were no such things as ghosts or spirits.
No-one had truly seen a Ghost or proved their existence. People with a good imagination probably believed they had seen a vision of some description and convinced other like-minded people that they had seen something.
Hogan had disproved many ghost stories, over the years, and had stayed in many "haunted houses" on his own, up and down the country, without seeing so much as a puff of a spirit.
"Ghosts" were a romantic distraction, invented by some lonely sad old bastards, who had nothing better to do. And if they ever did come across such a thing, they would shit themselves and run home screaming for their long-dead Mother.
The local radio station had interviewed him many times. As sightings were reported, they would call him into the studio, not only so he could disprove them, but to have a one on one with the person who supposedly saw the "Ghost" this was by far, the radio's busiest time.

Everyone enjoyed listening to Hogan upsetting the callers, who were convinced that they had seen a ghost. But it wasn't just the spirit world that suffered his denouncements.

Religion was also in the firing line for similar reasons; he had always maintained that "If he saw it, he would believe it"

'How could anyone seriously expect me to believe in something that I haven't seen? And millions of other people had not seen.'

He believed firmly in the power of the mind, and his "God", if there ever was such a thing, was in his mind. when something went wrong, he would ask his God for help, very occasionally it worked, but oft times it didn't. "But that is down to my inexperience, and not concentrating hard enough" was his argument.

'One day I will overcome this inexperience of Mind management and will be fully able to control the power that lies inert in the recesses of my brain, and then, maybe I will teach others how to do it. This will stop all talk of ghosts, spirits, and all religious visions, then everyone will know that I have been right all along. That Ghosts are purely a figment of one's imagination.'

That was the "Power of the mind" according to Jimmy Hogan.

Chapter One.

Hogan was sound asleep, he had spent the last four days and nights, in a supposedly haunted Pub.
He had seen nothing and heard even less, it was a private job that had been paid for by the owner of the Pub, Sonny Dixon.
He was a bit of a jack the lad in the Luton area and wanted everyone to know that he was the main man.
He usually had the biggest acts in his oversized pub, which was slap bang in between an industrial estate, and an ever-growing council estate.
Sonny Dixon had been more than a little upset that Hogan found that there was not a sign of ghosts, spirits, or suchlike residing in his pub.
Dixon was disillusioned with the bad news. He had been banking on ghosts because business was slow of late, and a real haunted Pub meant extra customers. But alas there was nothing.
He was so confident that Hogan would find a spirit other than what sat in the optics, that he had arranged for the local tv and radio stations to be there at Hogan's triumphant exit. But it was not to be.

The landlord paid him for the job that he had done and offered him a lot of money to say that there were ghosts and Evil entities on the property.
But Hogan, in his defence, would not tell lies and end up becoming something he despised. A hypocrite.
But he did agree not to tell anyone, as long as his name was not mentioned. So, the pub landlord got in touch with the papers and claimed it was haunted.
Oddly enough the papers had asked Hogan to go to the pub and check it out, he refused, and they managed to get another "Ghost hunter" to verify that the pub was indeed haunted. And they did.
Hogan laughed when he heard, knowing that Person had obviously been bribed, it wasn't the first time and it surely would not be the last time, it was a profitable business for shysters.
Hogan heard the phone ringing and thought that he was dreaming, but it didn't stop. He opened his eyes and looked at the clock, 05-35.
He picked up the phone and said, 'whoever this is? had better have a good reason for waking me up in the middle of the night.'
'I do apologise' said the female voice, 'I am looking for a James Hogan'
'Well you have found him, who is this?' he said sharply,
'Hi, my name is Geraldine Gilligan, and I work for a small independent television company called "Detection TV" We would like to hire your services for a couple of weeks, you will be suitably rewarded.'
'And what exactly would you like to suitably reward me for, Miss Gilligan?'

'Well we are developing a new ghost hunting programme, and we have found a house that is reportedly haunted by a violent spirit. We need you to check this house out and see if this spirit exists and if so, find out how dangerous it is?'

Hogan stifled a laugh, and threw his arms up in the air, 'Yes more easy money' he thought to himself.

'Well Miss Gilligan, I need to see something in writing like a contract and I will tell you how much I want, and a guarantee of payment, if there are no spirits, which I'm sure, will be the case. So when, and where would you like to meet me?'

'I was hoping to come to your place now and go through a contract with you, it has already been agreed with my bosses, and I am sure you will be agreeable with the financial package offered.

So, can I come and get this sorted out straight away because it is urgent, and if you agree, we want you in the house today.'

'Can I just ask you, Miss Gilligan, am I the first person that you have contacted about this Haunted house?'

'Yes, of course, Mr Hogan, your reputation as an honest investigator was the deciding factor, and actually, of all the names that we had gathered from an independent source your name is ten times more popular than your nearest rival, and please don't ask me who that is Mr Hogan, so can I call on you now?'

He had an idea who his "Nearest Rival" was. He agreed to see her and gave her his address. He told her not to rush because he needed a shower and would need to check his kit. To which she agreed.

He put the phone down and then prepared himself for her arrival. He packed a small holdall with clothes and toiletries, enough to last him for two weeks.

He also packed his special tool bag which had a large variety of electronic gadgets which he had collected over the years. It was comprised mainly of different electronic power gauges.

These would tell him if anyone was using electric power of any description, to try and fool him into believing that he could see so-called apparitions and things that went bump in the night.

Some of these gadgets he had invented himself and had them patented, and when he had retired from the ghost hunting/denouncing business, he would hopefully take them to a manufacturer and have them mass produced. That would give him a nice little retirement present, but that was in the future, this is now.

The doorbell rang, and he answered it straight away. He opened the door and gasped, she was nothing like he had imagined.

She stood there with a large briefcase, and an even larger smile, she was much younger than he thought, and she was very beautiful.

She smiled and introduced herself, and her colleague Danny Winters, who was standing behind her.

He ushered them into the living room and offered them refreshments, which they had both declined.

'First of all, I would like to know why this is so urgent, and why it couldn't have been done at a more civil time.'

He looked at her with a smile and raised his eyebrows waiting for an answer.
She looked at him and again she smiled.
'We have been working on this project for a few weeks, trying to negotiate with the owner of the house for a suitable time frame when we can take over the property for a couple of weeks.
The owner Mr Mullins wanted us to wait until his holidays in two months' time. Unfortunately, or fortunately for us, he phoned us yesterday evening claiming his wife was thrown down the stairs, by "an angry spirit."
She had suffered multiple fractures and was in the hospital. He told us we could have it until his wife is released from the hospital, and then they will go on holiday. On their return, he is going to have the builders in to demolish the house.
When we move out the demolition men will move In.'
She showed him the contract and gave him a cheque three times more than he was going to ask for, he willingly signed the contract after he examined it thoroughly.
'I noticed on the contract that you have installed or are in the process of installing cameras and various other forms of recording machines and will be locking me in the property.
I'm not worried but there is a health and safety issue here, so I would like there to be some sort of emergency exit, in case of fire.'
'That, of course, has already been sorted out Mr Hogan, we would not dream of locking you in without a secure exit, and besides, it is an insurance requisite,

and pictures have been taken of the entire house so that we are completely covered for any eventuality. Would there be anything else that you wish to discuss Mr Hogan? Even though you have signed the contract. You have the right to cancel anytime before you actually enter the building in question. Now, are we good to go Mr Hogan.'

'That was the only issue Miss Gilligan, and as it is being taken care of, there are absolutely no other problems at all, it's not my money that's being wasted' he said with a smirk.

'I think that when you are in that house you will agree that it will not be a waste of money. I feel that this house will change your whole outlook on life, and death, Mr Hogan, and our cameras will be there to record you as your life changes.

I firmly believe that there are spirits in that house, I have been in it and felt a presence there.

But you, Mr Hogan, are convinced that there is nothing there, and therefore have nothing to fear. So, prove it, and let the world share the outcome.' she returned the smirk.

Hogan looked her up and down while she was talking and thought how lovely she was, and she had a mind of her own, he was impressed with her.

'I really like this woman, apart from having a perfect body, and a very pretty face; there was something special about her.' He thought to himself.

He couldn't put his finger on it, but there was something there.

Hogan had had a few girlfriends, but they never stayed around for long, because of his constant commitment to disprove the existents of ghosts. So, he was nearly always away, not exactly the most romantic situation for them to be in. It seemed that most of them were believers of some description or "Romantics without cause" as he called them, so they never hung around too long.

He would like to find someone on his own wavelength, and maybe just as eager as he was to disprove sightings, but he knew that would never happen. Casual relationships were all he had to look forward to.

Miss Gilligan put the contract away and couldn't resist a sharp quip at Him.

'I wish you luck Mr Hogan, and I hope you pay as much attention to the job at hand, as you have paid to me. If you are ready your carriage awaits.'

He looked at her and smiled his best smile, and thought, 'definitely something special about her.'

The journey to the "haunted house" took only twenty minutes, and it was situated just northeast of Luton, on the A6 towards Bedford.

The car had been driven by Danny, who had said very little, he was a big guy, and Hogan assumed he was some sort of bodyguard?

He didn't think that he was linked romantically to Geraldine, there was nothing that he could see to prove otherwise. Danny had done what she told him to do that was it, nothing more nothing less.

Geraldine sat in the front passenger seat beside Danny and was making various phone calls to her boss, and the film crew, she reminded the film crew about the emergency exit.

Hogan wasn't really listening to her as she made the phone calls, he was just looking at her face. she had a few freckles on her nose, she had small dimples in her cheeks which emphasised her whole face, even more, when she smiled, which added to her attractiveness. Hogan decided that when this job was over, he would ask her to dinner. He also thought that maybe it was time to get a proper job and settle down, He knew that if he found the right girl Marriage and a family were a strong possibility.

Geraldine spoke to Him

'As far as the film crew go, they will under no circumstances enter the house, all their cameras are remotely controlled. Once you spot or observe a spirit or any form of activity, just talk into your microphone, and the cameras will zoom in on the subject or area. Are there any questions before you go into the house?'

There were no questions about the house, he very nearly asked her to dinner but stopped himself. This was the wrong time, best to wait until the two weeks are up. He would take her if she agreed to, one of the Old posh restaurants Probably in Harpenden. A small village near Luton on the south side. He could well afford it now.

He never noticed before because of his attraction to Geraldine, but he was in a big farmyard, there were two rather large houses. One of them was an older type probably early Victorian he thought. and a newer modern house that didn't look all that old, two maybe three years old.

He looked back at the older house and started walking towards it, looking all over for anything that would move or rattle, he would then discount any noise from these, it saves time.

Geraldine called after him, 'Where are you going?'

'Im going towards the house and was going to have a quick look around.'

'Well Mr Hogan, you are going the wrong way, it's the other house.'

'You got to be joking me, that house is only a few years old,'

'Eighteen months old,' to be exact, she answered.

Hogan became uneasy and suspicious, he felt that this was going to be some sort of set up by the television company, to try and discredit him.

He then noticed all the camera's, they were everywhere.

There were camera's facing every window of the house, there were cameras that were stood back from the house looking towards the windows and external walls.

He counted twelve cameras just in the front, he walked around the building there were another sixteen cameras placed around the rear and sides of the house,

He said to Geraldine,

'I think I have changed my mind, take me home I have suddenly just lost interest.'

'So, Mr Hogan do I detect fear in you, have you suddenly felt the power emanating from that house? I will, of course, cancel the contract, if you are that feared Mr Hogan?'

He looked at her, he had changed his mind about her, big time, and was glad he never asked her on a date. shrugging his shoulders, he changed his mind and would accept the inevitable.

He would have to be on guard the whole time. And of course, he was aware of some of the stunts these television companies could pull, to get record viewings.

'Ok let's get started' he said.

'I have to go in with you and show you where everything is, and do a voice test for the mike's,'

He again shrugged his shoulders and said 'Whatever'

They toured the building, it was a very large modern five-bedroom house, with all top of the range modern furnishings.

The kitchen was a large farmhouse type kitchen, purposely built, which he thought looked out of place, but again every mod con was fitted.

She gave him a diagram of the camera positions.

'There are off switches on the bathroom cameras for your privacy, but make sure you switch them back on after you have finished.'

She pointed out the emergency exit and opened it up to reveal a lovely flowered garden with so many different varieties of flowers and shrubs, a kaleidoscope of different colours, and smells.

'This garden is a well-established garden and is a lot older than this house and must be something to do with the old house?' he thought to himself.

She closed the door rather hurriedly as if trying to stop something coming in or getting out?

'Are there any questions? Mr Hogan.' She looked at him, he didn't look at her, he just answered 'no,'
'I know what you are thinking' she said. He looked at her and said.
'Oh, you do, and what exactly am I thinking Miss Gilligan?'
'Please call me Geraldine, you are thinking that this is a setup, aren't you?'
'Whatever gave you that idea, Geraldine?' he sneered
'I can't think of any other reason why you would want to cancel this investigation, but believe me, Mr Hogan this is one hundred per cent Kosher. You will find that out because you are naturally curious, and you will do your utmost to find the cause of anything you hear or see. That is why we chose you, simply because you are the best, so If that is all Mr Hogan, I will leave you to it, Happy ghost hunting.'
She went through the emergency exit and slammed the door shut.
He walked over to it and tested it, it opened easily enough, he closed it again.

Hogan went into the bathroom.
He turned the camera on and off, and then he started a serious examination of the house, examining floorboards, tapping walls, and double checking anything that could cover a "surprise".
The search took him six hours, such was his thoroughness for detail, but he had found nothing.

He memorised and measured where every Item of furniture and nik naks were. And would check it all over again tomorrow?

He looked at the large clock on the living room wall, it was still early two pm, he went into the kitchen and found some food and cooked himself a meal, and he looked at a camera, and said.

'I forgot to mention food, but will pay for anything I eat, in case you want to keep a note of everything, which I'm sure you will.'

A voice boomed back from a speaker on top of the fridge, 'There is no charge sir, compliments of Detection TV.'

Hogan had no idea who owned the voice and didn't really care. He washed up after himself and went into the lounge, and then he decided to do another Check and see if anything had changed?

He was very thorough and kept going from room to room, hoping to catch out if someone had made any slight changes, but found nothing.

He went into the kitchen made a coffee and grabbed a couple of biscuits, and then he returned to the living room.

He glanced at the clock it was just after six pm, he sat down, picked up a remote control and flicked on the TV, and started watching a western movie which he had seen before so many times, his eyes got heavy and he drifted off into a deep sleep.

He was woken by loud whispering, he opened his eyes and the whispering stopped, it was pitch black,
He stood up and searched around for and found the light switch. The TV had been switched off and

unplugged while he slept, he made a mental note of which way the TV cable was, just in case.

Something or someone passed by very close to him, he pretended not to notice, assuming it was the start of the setup pranks.

It had suddenly got very cold in the room, he started to shiver, he looked for the heating thermostat, found it and turned the temperature up a few degrees, it was set at zero.

'but even so, it shouldn't be that cold he thought to himself.'

A thought came to him that maybe the crew had an underground cold air blower somewhere, which would rapidly drop the temperature, again he decided to ignore it, and would double check the air vents and the floorboards in the morning.

'If they want to try and frighten me, they are going to have their work cut out' he said to himself. A voice broke the silence. 'Is there anything to report Mr Hogan?' the voice asked.

'No, nothing to report, situation normal'

'O.K. please keep us in the loop.'

Hogan hated that saying, some stupid American saying borne out of the yuppie era.

He didn't answer just walked into the kitchen and made a cup of tea, he looked for and found some more biscuits.

He took the tea and biscuits into the lounge, he plugged in the TV and put the news station on, 'nothing much happening in the world.' He said aloud,

'What was that Mr Hogan?' the voice asked,
'Nothing, I just farted'
'O.k.' said the voice; there's medication in the kitchen if you need it.'
'Cheers and in future, if anyone is talking to me, could you say your name, I could be having a conversation with a robot, which would do nothing for my street cred, and just call me Hogan. If you could make a note of that?'
'Yes, of course, my name is Robin and I will be here till six am, and then Juliet will take over from me.'
'Thank you, Robin, I don't think I will need you anymore tonight, but you will know if I do.'
he heard the microphone click off and he smiled.
'One has to show willing I suppose' he thought.
He finished his tea and biscuits, then went for a shower, he felt so much better, he proceeded to search out the bedrooms.

He picked one of the larger bedrooms, it was an en suite, which suited him. He looked at the bed and looked underneath it and underneath the mattress, there was nothing hidden.

He pulled the bed away from its spot by about four foot, just in case, there was anything under the floorboards that could move the bed while he was asleep. He would take no chances.

There was a book on the bedside cabinet, it was a romantic woman's book, called the Angel who loved. He threw it under the bed.

He picked up his holdall and took out a writing pad, he would make a note of everything they threw at him. He made a few notes and looked at the time, it was eleven forty-five.

He thought to himself that if anything was going to happen it would happen in the next fifteen minutes, 'because everyone associated midnight with strange unexplained happenings'

He plugged in his own bedside lamp with a long cable and an on/off switch, which he kept in his hand.

He laid down on the bed and started thinking about the house next door it was a lovely old house so full of character, it certainly seemed strange that they had never used that house for the setup?

'Maybe it was full of expensive antiques, and the production company couldn't get insurance for the house, hmm very strange,' he thought, he looked at the clock 01-15.

'Perhaps everything is going to happen tomorrow?'
He started to drift off, and then felt a cold hand on his face gently stroking up and down, he had the lamp switch in his hand and turned it on.

For a brief second, he saw a faint outline of a woman's face inches away from his face, and then she was gone! He could still feel the coldness and a tingling feeling on his face.

'How the hell did they do that?' he asked himself. He looked around but tried not to make it too obvious.

'Hi Hogan, its Robin, is everything all right?'
'No problem Robin,' he lied, 'just remembered an appointment with the dentist I forgot about.'
'They are pretty clever, I can't quite get my head around how they did that, there has to be some sort of projection machine in the wall?'

He made a mental note of roughly the direction the projection would have come from. He turned off the light and waited for something to happen, but nothing did, he eventually drifted off to sleep as dawn broke.

He woke up at eight fifteen and decided to have a good look around before he took a shower.
He double checked everything that he saw last night, it all seemed to be ok, he checked all the doors and windows, using his gadgets, but found nothing, the kitchen was his next port of call, he flicked on the kettle.
'Good morning Mr Hogan, my name is Juliet and I will be here if you need me, just call my name and I will answer straight away.'
'Good morning to you too Juliet, and thank you, we will see how the day goes.'
'What a nice pleasant voice' He thought to himself, 'A much better personality than Robin, and a sexier voice.' He laughed to himself.
He made himself a coffee, and some toast at the same time looking very closely for any signs of anything out of the ordinary. He finished his toast and coffee, washed up and then went into the bathroom.
He stripped off and got into the large walk-in shower then remembered the cameras; he covered himself and turned them off.
He stood in the shower with his head leaning against the wall, enjoying the heat and the pulsating power of the shower.

He was a little stiff, but the shower felt like an invigorating massage, he was in no hurry to move and relished every luxurious second.

He opened his eyes and thought that he saw a movement in his peripheral vision, he looked around but saw nothing, the floor was wet but there were no footprints.

He returned to his previous position with his head against the wall.

He started to wash and was about to start singing when all of a sudden someone punched him hard twice in his kidneys. He collapsed onto his knees the pain was so intense, he briefly saw something transparent standing over him under the shower, he couldn't make out what it was, and then it moved out of the shower and disappeared, there was a trail of strange shaped footprints leading out through a solid wall.

He laid there until the pain eased, he struggled to his feet, and the pain came shooting back. Struggling, he opened the bathroom door; he was naked but was in too much pain to worry, he tried to make it into the kitchen.

The strange figure came back and stood in front of him and laughed, it was the most frightening noise he had ever heard in his life. The figure was more of an apparition, like a vapour cloud, or something similar. He felt a sudden hard punch to his chest, he found it hard to breathe, he was gasping for air, he felt helpless, and something inside his mind told him that he was dying.

He could do nothing to help himself; slowly the darkness enveloped him, He could hear the eerie cackling laughter, which seemed to follow him on his journey to death.

Chapter two.

Hogan nervously opened his eyes, the pain had gone, although his head was feeling a bit woozy, he saw the ground far below fast disappearing into the distance. he was floating miles above the ground, there was nothing supporting him, no vehicles and no oxygen how could this be?
He turned over and saw a pitch-black sky above him. He recognised the stars and planets of the solar system, far off in the distance, he saw a bright light, it was fast approaching him.
He soon realised that it was he who was moving towards the light and at an ever-increasing speed.
And then he remembered the pain that he suffered, someone had attacked him, and now he was dead, heading towards the gates of St Peter.
Hogan was sad, there was so much in life that he still wanted to do, he shouldn't be here it was so unfair.
He reflected on his past life as it presented itself to him in little video shows.
he had made a few errors in judgement in his earlier life, but since then he had tried to be honest and virtuous.

He may have unintentionally upset a few people in his professional life but overall, he wasn't a great sinner.
He hoped that would put him in favour when he was being judged, by whoever it is who picks the souls destination.
He was getting very much closer to the bright light ahead; he strained his eyes trying to visualise exactly what it was, then he noticed that there were other people flying past him at a greater speed, he tried talking to them, but they ignored him, he looked around, there were hundreds of people heading towards the ever-nearing light, and all at different speeds.

Something burning went flying past him heading in the opposite direction, he looked around and saw more, many more and they were all making a high-pitched screaming noise.
He looked closer at the burning objects and realised that they were people! He heard their ear-shattering screams and saw their faces, contorted by the pain of their burning bodies, caused he believed by their re-entry into the earth's atmosphere.
Hogan started panicking as he realised that the burning bodies were being despatched straight to hell, and they were being warmed up for their journey so that they could acclimatise and would not change hell's temperature when they arrived, Damnation was a hard punishment.

He was almost at the entrance to the bright light, there was an orderly queue, nobody wanted to push in and force the choice of the Judge.
As each person arrived at the gate, they pressed a bell to announce themselves, now it was his turn to press the bell, heaven or hell? He closed his eyes... and pressed the bell.
He felt himself moving on a travellator, he opened his eyes and saw millions of people heading in millions of different directions in groups of fours on their own travellator, it was like looking through some sort of kaleidoscope, he looked behind him and saw that there were three people standing there smiling, he tried to talk to them but he couldn't move his mouth, he knew then that he too was smiling. After a while, it got boring, a bit like being on a bus ride that you made every day of the year, boring... Boring... Boring.

But then something started happening ahead of him, and he didn't like what he saw. All of a sudden, the millions of people started to disappear, and in a downward direction, in flames.
A ghostly hand picked out either one, two, three or all four of the people standing smiling on their travellator. He felt the people panicking behind him, he looked around and saw two of his fellow passengers burst into flames and were thrown out of the travellator in a downward direction. He looked at the other passenger and he was unsure whether it was male or female, even though it was naked, as was he.

He looked down at his groin area and noticed that there was nothing there, absolutely nothing, it resembled a naked doll that he used to see in the street or thrown onto a dustbin, his ideas of reincarnation just took a nose dive.

The travellator was still moving whichever way, there was no way of telling which way was which. But at least for the moment, he was safe although there were many flaming bodies flying past him and his passenger, a few of them had crashed into his transport and bits of burning body flew everywhere, if he could have screamed, he would have been hoarse by now.

Suddenly the transport stopped dead and turned around, he saw in the distance a light the size of a pinhole, and that was difficult because of the flying flaming bodies, but it was getting bigger, slowly but surely.

After what seemed forever the flaming bodies disappeared, and the white light started to get bigger quicker.

All of a sudden, the transport picked up speed and headed towards the light at a breath-taking, heart stopping, million miles an hour.

It arrived at some sort of docking station and stopped at an ice cream stall.

A woman with blond hair and the reddest lips that he had ever seen in his life beckoned him and his companion out of the travellator and sat them both down at a multicoloured table and filled it up with hundreds of different flavours of ice cream.

She stuck a giant handbell in the middle of the ice cream covered table and pointed at it and then pointed at her watch several times.
He failed to understand what she was saying, but his fellow Passenger who had not stopped stuffing the Ice cream was feeling decidedly ill.
It… whatever it was picked up the bell and started ringing it violently. So much so that Hogan's nose started bleeding. He fell off the chair and onto the floor, he saw his companion gradually getting weaker and the bell gradually slowed down.
Hogan gratefully closed his eyes and started to drift off to sleep but was aware of the bell, that suddenly changed its pitch.

He heard a slow but continuous BEEP-BEEP-BEEP, he opened his eyes slowly, bright lights were all around him, he was going back to heaven, he blinked, unsure of where he was, then he smelt the unmistakable smell of a hospital.
He tried to sit up but was prevented from doing so by somebody he couldn't see.
'No more ice cream, please, take it away… please.'
'It's ok Hogan you are in a hospital, don't move till I get someone' he couldn't see who it was, but he thought he recognised the voice.
'Geraldine is that you?' there was silence, then he heard running footsteps in a corridor of some sort? There was silence for a few seconds, and then he heard the echoes bouncing off the walls they came closer and closer and then they stopped, someone close to him was breathing heavy.

'My name is doctor Shallell, can you hear me?'
'Yes' replied Hogan 'I know I am in a hospital, what happened?'
'We understand that you were attacked, and mugged, this young lady beside me, found you and brought you here, and it's a good job she did, she saved your life.'
'I want to sit up.' the doctor helped him to sit up, slowly his vision cleared, he saw Geraldine standing beside the doctor, she smiled at him, he could see through the smile, there was some sort of sadness in her face.
'The police would like a statement from you to find out what happened, this young lady stumbled on you, there was no one else around, do you remember anything?' The doctor asked.
Hogan looked at Geraldine and saw the worried look on her face,
'I don't remember anything at all, so there's no need for the police; I never had much money on me so it's hardly worth the bother.'
'Well, be that as it may, you can tell that to the police, you suffered a very vicious attack and had to undergo an emergency operation. One of your ribs had broken and pierced your lung, and your heart had stopped beating several times, you have been here for four weeks.
We have just brought you out of an induced coma because you are now strong enough and you are healing satisfactorily. We still need to do more tests on you before you will be allowed home, I just need your name and a few other details.

I will leave you in the company of this young lady, who, I may hasten to add, has been to see you every day since you were brought in, her name is Miss Geraldine Gilligan, and your name is?'
'Hogan, Jimmy Hogan,'
'Well Mr Hogan, May I introduce you to Miss Gilligan, I will leave you together to get acquainted I'll be back in five minutes to get all your details.'
The Doctor left the room humming some sort of unknown tune, he went straight to a nurse at the nurse's station and pointed towards Hogan's room, she started taking notes and nodding her head.
They were looking at a computer and both writing down various bits of information, and then the nurse made a phone call and started chatting away to whoever.
'Well hello Miss Gilligan, would you like to tell me what I'm really doing here? Did one of your pranks go wrong?'
'You really don't remember what happened?' she asked,
'The last I remember was someone touching my face in bed; I haven't worked out how you did that but give me time.' He smiled sardonically.
'Mr Hogan Please, believe me, we are not setting you up or pulling pranks, all we know, and this is on video is that you came out of the bathroom and collapsed.
I had to perform CP on you to start your heart, we dressed you and brought you straight to this hospital. they lost you a few times, and we're going to give up

on you, but thank god they finally managed to get you back.
I made up the story about you getting mugged because we would lose millions if this got out. Unfortunately, we never took out the correct insurance. But Mr Hogan you will still get paid, in fact, your pay has trebled. And as long as you are incapacitated, we will foot the bill, so you are perfectly welcome to milk this as long as you like.'
He looked at her, and tried to imagine what she was thinking? What was going on in her pretty head?
'So, Miss Gilligan, you being here at my bedside had nothing to do with you being worried about me? You just didn't want me to say what happened when I recovered, so what's to stop me blabbing the truth?'
'You can "blab" as you put it, if you so wish, it won't change the pay deal we have given you, it's been nice meeting you, Mr Hogan, we shall not be seeing each other again, goodbye!!!'
'Wait, Geraldine, don't go I really don't remember anything, I need your help,' She stopped in the doorway just as a uniformed policeman was about to knock the door.
'Hello Mr Hogan, my name is Constable John Galloway, I've come to get a statement from you,' Hello Miss Gilligan, it's nice to see you again, he continued.
'I couldn't help overhearing you say you don't remember anything, is that really the case? Maybe there is something sir? No matter how small, that would help us catch these people.
'I'm sorry constable I have just been talking to the

lovely Miss Gilligan, trying to remember, and there is nothing at all, but if I do remember even the slightest detail, I will make sure you get that information.
So, if you would excuse me, I would like to continue thanking Miss Gilligan for saving my life.'
The constable walked out of the room, smiling at Geraldine. 'Thank you, Miss Gilligan,' he said.
'Could you come in and close the door please Geraldine.' Hogan pleaded. She hesitated briefly then sighed and closed the door, she sat on the chair furthest away from his bed.
'What is it?' she asked.
'Well there are one or two points that need clarifying'
'And what exactly are they?'
I'm surprised really that I remember anything at all and that's what surprises me.
You say this is not a setup, but the first night someone or something touched my face, and it tingled for a while, can't actually describe it but very similar to toothpaste on the tongue, so can you explain that? And as I have said I really do not remember coming out of the bathroom, so I really would like an explanation of that incident and exactly why I am here?'
'I really have no explanation for anything, let me go back and watch the videos again, and see what I can come up with, that is the best I can do, I have no answers, we were relying on you to give us the answers we need.'
'Just who exactly is "we" 'He asked her,
'The whole television company belongs to my father,

we have had some lean times recently and we were hoping that a true haunted house would help us.
On the good side we have in the can, ready and waiting to televise, a full list of people who are known conmen and women, pretending they are mediums with the power to attract ghosts etc.
This is your field of expertise, and we were going to ask you to present the forthcoming series, and expose as many people as possible?
But this house came up and as I have said I have a feeling that this is the real thing, so we think whatever happened to you, is the same thing that happened to the lady of the house.'
'So, you want me to believe that it was some sort of "spirit" that put me in here? Which goes against everything I believe in, and spent my life trying to disprove?'
'Do you have any other explanation?' She asked.
He never answered, the doctor knocked on the door and came in.
Geraldine made her excuses and left, she gave Hogan a long lingering look, then she was gone.
Hogan spent the next few hours having blood tests and all the other tests that cause pain and discomfort, to see if one is feeling any better.
He bravely ignored the pain of the tests, all he could think about was Geraldine, and could it be possible that there were spirits or just some elaborate cover-up?
When all the testing was finished, they made him comfortable and left him alone with his thoughts. He

started dropping off, and then he suddenly remembered the shower and the pain.

He remembered everything. The hairs on his neck and arms stood up, he started shaking and the pain that he first felt came back with a vengeance.

He managed to press the emergency button the nurses came running in, he could hear voices around him but could see nothing, then the darkness came, slowly at first, the pain eased, the voices stopped, at last, the darkness came.

Hogan opened his eyes slowly and blinked, the lights were bright, he struggled to look around then he saw Geraldine's smiling face, 'Are you an angel?' He asked with a smile on his face.

'If I was, I would have died of boredom long ago, you have been asleep for two days, and here I am, sat here like a lemon.'

'A very pretty lemon though, and its one of my favourite colours'

'Well Mr Hogan, I have some news that will wipe that grin off your face, firstly I have checked through the videos from that night, and you are not going to like this.

The master switch for the bathroom was left on, it should have been switched off as soon as you turned the switch on the camera off, but it recorded you in the shower, and it clearly shows some sort of apparition, for want of a better word, in the shower with you.

The power of the water made it visible in places, and even better, if you'll forgive me, it clearly shows you

being hit, when you go down the apparition is standing over you.
I have the whole thing on my laptop, and, the first night you got into bed, there is another apparition sitting on your bed, it looks like a naked female, but we couldn't really say for certain.'
She gave him time to take in what she had told him, he sat there with his mouth open, saying nothing, and then he started shaking his head.
She took out her laptop and switched it on, she set up the video and passed it to Jimmy, and he looked at the video and replayed it about five or six times.
'That doesn't prove anything, I've had better than that and threw it out because it was made up.'
'That video is not made up, that is a true copy from your attack, and I resent you giving it the big I am at other peoples expense,' she got up and was making her way to the door.'   He shouted after her,
'That is exactly how I remember it.'
She stopped in her tracks, turned around and looked at him, he pointed to the chair beside his bed, and she sat down and raised her eyebrows waiting to hear more.
'The other night after you left, I was about to drop off, and then suddenly everything came back to me, including the pain, I can still see the strange shape of a face, and still, feel the pain, and as for the naked woman? I caught a very small glimpse of her face. But I thought it was the start of the setup, now I am totally confused.
My whole life has been about proving that this really doesn't happen, and I'm sure I didn't imagine it, or

self-inflicted this pain upon myself.'

'You can take that laptop to whomever you want, to check the video, and we will supply the original if you need it.

We have nothing to hide, your job has now finished Mr Hogan, as I said before you have no money worries, as long as you are incapacitated.

And as far as the house goes, we have a new "Ghost hunter" going into the house tonight. You may have seen her on the television? Madelyn Clarke, she is very highly rated, and has seen more than a few spirits in her time.'

'From an optic stand,' Hogan said.

'They are the only spirits she has ever seen; she is a con artist. If you would have checked back, you would have found that I have proved she set up all the happenings on her programme, but because she is big time no one believed me.'

'We have checked up, Mr Hogan, we saw all the evidence that you produced, and the lady in question has refuted your claim, and threatened to sue you if you proceeded with your accusations, that's why you never took it any further because she could have financially ruined you.'

'It's all down to money in the end, but ok, that's your choice, let her go into the house. And if you want, I will write down exactly what she will say as soon as she sets foot inside that house, word for word.

Her whole life is a script, choreographed from the moment she opens her eyes to the time she closes them at night.

But I suppose that sounds like sour grapes to you, so go ahead and good luck.
I really mean that and make sure your insurance covers every eventuality, I would hope to see you again, Geraldine, but I know that's not going to happen.'
'You never know what's around the corner Mr Hogan, there is an address stuck to the laptop. When you have finished with it, could you possibly send it to that address? Thank You, Mr Hogan, it's been a pleasure meeting you, I wish you all the luck in the future, Goodbye.'
She turned and walked straight out the door, not looking back, Hogan sat there with his mouth open, trying to think of something to say to get her back, but there was nothing.
He suddenly felt lonely for the first time in his life, he kept staring at the open door hoping she would return but nothing.

He opened her laptop and watched the video, again and again, he closed it and asked a nurse if she could get him some paper and a pen. When she returned, he started writing and didn't stop until he had finished and was sure that he had never missed out anything.
He put the writing inside the laptop, and then he used the hospital phone and called a courier, who came straight away and picked up the laptop. He placed it into a secure bag then sealed it in front of Him, it would be delivered within the hour.

Hogan then made another call, to the recipient of the laptop, telling him, that it was on the way, and urgency was the order of the day.

He laid down and closed his eyes, the darkness came, and he drifted off.

Hogan was tired and didn't want to open his eyes, but he sensed there were people in the room with him, finally he opened his eyes and saw there were about eight or nine people standing around the bed looking at him.

He sat up and looked at each one of them in turn. 'Who are you?' he asked the nearest person, 'are you the police? I don't remember anything I've told you, now please go away.'

'We are not Police jimmy" have a good look do you not recognise any of us? take your time.'

Hogan looked at them again but didn't know any of them. 'I'm afraid you are complete strangers, I don't know you, and I have never seen any of you before, so could you please go and find someone else to bother.'

'You are the person we have come to see, Jimmy. I am your Father, Jack Hogan, this is your Mother, Grace, your Grandfather James, and your great grandfather, great uncles, and aunties. We are your family Jimmy and now you can finally see us.

I know there is so much you want to ask us, and so much we have to tell, we can't make up for never being there for you. Unfortunately, our lives were unfairly cut short.'

Hogan looked at them all, he never noticed before, but they were all dressed differently.

Their Clothes were dated and different, He felt around for the panic button, he found it and pressed it repeatedly, he looked behind him and saw the light flashing at the nurse's station and two nurses ran towards him.

He turned towards the strangers, but they had disappeared. The two nurses came in almost together, squeezing themselves through the doorway, and they looked at him expectantly.

'Is everything alright Mr Hogan, do you need any painkillers.'

'Who were those people?'

'Err what people Mr Hogan?'

'All those people that were in this room a couple of seconds ago, you must have seen them,' the nurses looked at each other and shook their heads.

'I'm afraid you must have been dreaming sir, there has been no one in your room since Miss Gilligan. Anyone that comes here has to go past the nurses' station, and because of your condition, you are always being monitored, sir. We must look in your direction every few minutes and make notes of your visible condition in the paperwork.

I think maybe you were dreaming; would you like a sleeping pill?'

Hogan looked at both the nurses, and apologised for calling them, he agreed with them and said he must have dreamt the whole thing.

They checked his temperature and blood pressure while they were there, he watched them go back to their station, and they kept looking at him and making notes.

He lay down and remembered what the stranger said about him being his father.

His parents were both killed just after he was born, and their names were Jack and Grace Hogan. There were no surviving relatives, so Hogan was adopted, and all he had to remember his parents was a single tattered wedding picture.

He was totally confused as to who these strangers were and unsure that he may have imagined it? But if not, what the hell was it that they wanted?

He decided they were probably con merchants, looking for an easy buck, he had seen them all too frequently. The faded wedding picture of his parents came floating back to him, there was definitely a resemblance to the stranger who spoke, and the woman he pointed to, his Mother 'pure coincidence' he thought. Once again sleep consumed him…….

Chapter Three.

Geraldine was in the television control room, checking that everything was set up and ready for Madelyn Clarke's arrival.
The Ghost hunter star had insisted on her own cameraman following her around the house.
Geraldine had vetoed the request, stating that the contract insisted only one person would be allowed to conduct the investigation as per the insurance requisite.
The real reason was to prevent any attempt to choreograph and compromise any findings; this was put into the contract after watching previous videos of the famous female Ghost hunter and as a direct response to Hogan's accusations.
She was alone in the control room, thinking about Hogan, she thought at first that he was an arrogant son of a bitch, but she had warmed to him, and she knew apart from his attitude he would always speak as he found.
He was, in fact, her sort of guy. She had one or two romances in the past that never came to anything because the men had tried to overly impress her. But she knew that her father's money was the real target.

She had never met a real man, Hogan was the closest to her ideal man, but she had decided never to see him in a romantic context, or any other context come to that, it just wasn't going to happen.

The monitors started flashing on and off, distorted whispering sounds started coming through the speakers.

She looked closely at the monitors, they all had snowy screens, and then a face appeared, it looked vaguely like a woman's face, and then it changed, it distorted into something unexplainable, something grotesque, and seemed to come out of the monitors towards her.

Geraldine froze, she couldn't move, she felt her chest slowly being constricted, the apparition came close and covered her face, her life force was being sucked out of her. The pain was unbearable her body was burning.

She saw a white light through the darkness and knew her time was near, she was drawn through the light and saw human shapes in the distance, they were waving to her, and calling her name.

And then suddenly she felt a force pulling her backwards, still, they called her name. 'Geraldine… Geraldine.

'Geraldine wake up,' Slowly she opened her eyes and saw Charlie the production manager, she struggled to breathe but couldn't, Charlie lifted her up and carried her outside.

There was loud cackling laughter coming through the sound system, Charlie breathed into her lungs and pumped her chest, she coughed then started to

breathe. it was very laboured; a first aid assistant gave her oxygen.
She sucked in as much of the life-giving gas as she could, gradually she started breathing normally, and she felt her strength returning slowly.
Finally, she came around and opened her eyes then saw all the production crew standing and staring at her, she tried to stand but was prevented from doing so by Charlie he told her to wait a minute or two before she moved.
Just at that moment, Madelyn Clarke's entourage turned up. Geraldine pushed Charlie away and stood up, Charlie just looked at her, she thanked him and asked him not to say anything in front of Ms Clarke, she assured him that she was ok. He left her reluctantly.
She brushed herself down and went across the yard to greet Madelyn Clarke. She could still hear the Demonic cackling laughter in her head.
The pain in her chest was easing but she would never ever forget it. The whole incident would haunt her for the rest of her life. However long that may be?
Madelyn Clarke shook Geraldine's hand and then wasted no time issuing demands, Geraldine showed her the contract and told her there would be no extras, and certainly no alcohol allowed on the premises under any circumstances.
Ms Clarke knew she would not gain anything from arguing with Geraldine, she signed the contract reluctantly, Geraldine asked her to re-read it before she signed so that they were both agreed in principle. There was also a disclaimer in case of any injuries

howsoever caused, this was also part of the agreement, and failure to sign would cancel the contract instantly.

This added clause was also as a direct result of Jimmy's "Accident" although nothing was mentioned about his part in the start of the investigation. Mostly because there was no love lost between the two, and Geraldine didn't want to cause any problems by providing a rod to be hit with.

She did, however, inform Ms Clarke that she had one hour to pull out if she was unsure of anything and that if she did, there would be no second chance.

Ms Clarke refused to take the hour Quoting, 'I am big enough and ugly enough to get myself into trouble, meaning, I know what I signed and I'm happy with the deal, now would you care to show me where I am staying.'

She, as did Hogan, started heading towards the old house, Geraldine pointed her in the right direction, she showed her the inside of the building and went through various tests on the microphones when all was done, she closed the door and left Ms Clarke to her own devices.

Hogan awoke from a deep natural sleep and felt totally refreshed, he was hungry and looked over to the nurse's station, there was no one there, he got out of bed, and gingerly tested his weight on the floor, he took a step but felt very light-headed. He started breathing deeply to try and clear the cobwebs. Slowly but surely, he felt more confident, he skirted the room hanging on to anything that was

convenient. He looked around, the place was empty and silent, there was nothing to hear.
There were no sounds that you would normally associate with a hospital.
He looked at the clock at the nurse's station it was eleven fifteen, obviously morning because the sun was shining through the big windows.
The warmth of the sun made him feel stronger, but he needed food, he looked around again all the ward beds were empty, he saw a double door ahead and went through, still no one to be seen.
He smelt food cooking and tried to follow the smell, suddenly he heard a crashing noise coming from a room just ahead of him.
There was no sign on the door, he opened the door, as he did so, he heard whispering. It was dark inside, he felt around and found a switch, the door slammed shut behind him, the light came on and he saw that there were four bodies on examination tables.
Two of the bodies on the tables sat up, Hogan took a few steps back and banged into the door hurting his already painful body.
The body nearest to him spoke. 'Don't worry mate, we can't hurt you, we're dead, my name is Duncan, and this is Fred, you must be lost cos this is the Morgue'
Hogan was speechless, he knew then that it was a dream and he would soon wake up, at least he hoped it was a dream.
He spoke to Duncan; he felt a bit daft doing so but he would wake up shortly.
'So, what actually happened to you guys?'

'So, what happened to you guys' Duncan mimicked.
'Dead, is what happened to us, a poxy multiple car smash, started off by Fred here talking to his broker on the phone. Worried about his shares and didn't give a fuck about where his car was going, and we are the result. Four mangled dead bodies.
And you Mate really believe you are dreaming, don't you? Well, Mr whatever your name is? You are wide awake, and you are talking to dead bodies, how does that grab you?'
'If I am wide awake where is everybody?'
'Fire practice, they are all outside, you must have been asleep, and they forgot about you? obviously not that important? Or they thought you were dead? They forget about us cos we are already dead meat, but we still have feelings.'
The other bodies in the room rolled about laughing.
There was a loud rasping noise.
'Was that you farting again Fred?'
'Yes, of course, it was me and it's a good sign because those medical experts reckon that if you are in hospital and you fart it is a sign you are getting better.'
'Fred you thick murdering bastard, they have taken all your insides out, there is nothing there! You are dead, like the proverbial Parrot, you are not going to get better, there is fuck all left to get better.'
'Why do you try and destroy everyone's dream you miserable bastard.' he said as he let another fart off.
'You destroyed all our dreams you fucking criminal when you made that phone call in your car.'

'Nothing like rubbing salt in the wounds, catch this you grumpy fucker.' Fred let off a major floor trembling fart, despite not having any insides. There was another loud bang, one of the other bodies' legs fell off the trolley on to the floor, 'Fred will you block your fucking arse up, it's not making anyone better, and you just blew my fucking legs off!' There was silence for a split second, and then hysterical laughter erupted from all his roommates.

Hogan was unsure whether to laugh or cry, he turned around and left the room, and continued his journey looking for food.

He heard a commotion, and then saw nurses and doctors come through a big set of doors, they were moaning about Fire practise being a waste of time. One of the nurses saw Hogan and grabbed hold of him and started to take him back to the ward, 'No!' he said, 'I'm hungry, I want some food,'

'Yes, Mr Hogan if we can get you back to your bed its lunchtime, we will get you some food.

The nurse helped him back into bed; he started thinking about his situation and was so certain that he was in a dream state.

A Nurse brought him a tray of food, he looked at it and then said to the nurse.

'I'm not dreaming this am I'

'No Mr Hogan, you are not dreaming,' She chuckled, 'I'm sure if you were dreaming you would have dreamt a better lunch than this?'

'That's exactly what I was thinking nurse.' she smiled and walked away, suddenly Hogan had lost his appetite.

He started to believe that maybe his life had changed, although there was no obvious reason to think that. He thought back to the strangers that surrounded his bed, and then the talking dead bodies in the morgue.

'Maybe I am going mad? Maybe I have always been mad?' He started questioning his whole life, he had proved that there were no such things as ghosts and exposed frauds to the police.

His whole life was about the truth as he saw it, he was paid to do a good job, so why did he now feel different? Then suddenly his mood changed, he saw his reflection in the glass and smiled.

'To be honest' he thought, 'I still can't say that I have actually seen a ghost and that maybe the things that I have seen, are as a result of being in here and the after-effects of the medication they have given me? So, I will not take any more medicine. I will get back to normal and be my happy disbelieving self.' He laughed.

How could I have thought even for a minute that I had seen anything that would have turned my life around, and made me any different?'

Hogan was on the road to recovery, and he was convinced that he hadn't changed, convinced that the visions he saw were inflicted as a result of the chemicals from the medication.

He decided to try and get discharged, he didn't want to walk out in case he got ill again and wouldn't be able to claim insurance.

He felt good and would pester the doctors to discharge him, he wanted his life back, he wanted to carry on doing what he was good at, getting rid of the shysters and conmen.
They are the scum of society, willingly ripping off people who had lost someone dear to them.
'Yes, Jimmy Hogan is back and ready to kick arse.'

Madelyn Clarke was all alone in the house, she was angry because one of the production staff had told her that Jimmy Hogan had been in the house a few weeks earlier and had a serious accident and that he was still in the hospital, but now out of danger.
She hated Hogan with a vengeance; he and his big mouth had cost her money, as a result of his investigations about her being a fraud.
She laughed to herself; of course, she was a fraud, who wasn't? There was plenty of money to be made by everyone, but Hogan wouldn't take a bribe.
She threatened him with court action, and she knew that she was lucky that he had never pursued his allegations.
She was advised not to push the issue by her agent, who told her, that if push came to shove, Jimmy Hogan would ruin her.
She was also lucky that Jimmy Hogan wasn't necessarily vindictive, but he was also nowhere near rich enough to call her bluff.
She surveyed the building wondering how she was going to pull anything out of the hat without her own cameraman, Tabors Zielinski.

She had come across him on a visit to Poland. He was, in fact, a magician, a multi-talented illusionist. And between them, they had fleeced several television companies using Their combined skills. No one had ever noticed, except Hogan. She had a natural sneer whenever she thought of that man.

As she looked around the house, she worked out what was going where from her box of tricks that she had smuggled in, along with a small two-way radio.

She could talk to her partner and cameraman Tabors, who would help and instruct her with any deception.

After mentally picturing the house she went to the bathroom and turned off the camera and sat down to talk to Tabors.

Tabors wasn't answering the phone. she knew he was sitting in the car less than forty feet away; she would try again later.

Meanwhile, she would give a running commentary, telling Geraldine where all the cold spots were, and make up some shit until she was ready to sort something out with Tabors.

Although she had a plan, she would always double check plausibility with the professional. She called Tabors twice more without success, she could wing it for a while if she really had to, she had done it before she met Tabors and was quite successful.

But Tabors was the master and added the much-needed polish that she sadly lacked.

The producers never had a clue what certain Mediums could and could not see. It was an art form that took years of practice and effrontery.

They just have to make it believable in front of the cameras, a certain degree of acting, showmanship, and professional distractions and illusions would certainly help the Medium portray what the viewer is looking for.

She turned the camera back on and left the bathroom, she then called Geraldine.

'Hello, Geraldine, are you there?'

'Yes, Madelyn we are receiving you loud and clear, are you going for practice or should we start recording straight away?'

'Well it's getting late, almost six pm so we may as well go for the kill if you pardon the pun, I hope you have sufficient microphones and cameras set up, I would hate you to miss something due to a shortage of equipment.'

'I can assure you, Ms Clarke, there are more than enough Microphones, we are even picking up the gentle beat of your heart'

'Okay let's go for it'

'Okay Madelyn on your countdown five to zero, the recorder starts at two speak at zero.'

'Don't try to teach your granny to suck eggs, princess, I am experienced, I have forgotten more than you will ever know.'

'Five, four, three, two, one, zero.' Madelyn started to walk around the Kitchen and was listening out for any sounds.

'Hello Madelyn, are you picking anything up?'

'Give me a chance child I have only just started, I... Shh did you hear that, oh my goodness there is a small child sitting on the floor by the kitchen sink he

is crying, can you hear that Geraldine?'
'Negative on that Madelyn none of the instruments are registering.'
'I'm going to get closer to the child, and...... oh He's gone straight through the wall, I really hope your videos picked the child up. That is the clearest spirit I have ever seen; this whole kitchen is full of cold spots.' Geraldine tried to speak with Madelyn several times but was shushed like a child being scolded.

The medium was supposedly talking to other spirits that she had just encountered, nothing was picked up by any of the expensive and sensitive instruments.
'I'm afraid I am exhausted Geraldine I need to stop to regain my strength, it is so tiring, I need a bathroom break, she shouted out, Cut!'
Geraldine signalled to the technicians to stop recording, she was not best pleased the cameramen needed a bit more warning, so they had time to tail off, and feather, it would make it easier to join up when she restarts.
'For future reference Madelyn I will tell you when to stop, I want a polished production.' Madelyn stuck her fingers up at the cameras as she made her way to the bathroom. She turned off the camera and sat down, she put her hand down her pants and produced a small flask containing whiskey. She took a swig and savoured the taste, then took another swig and replaced the flask to its hiding place. Then picked up her two-way radio and whispered. 'Are you there Tabors?' There was no answer.

'Tabors you had better answer me, or I'll kick your arse back to where I found you.' Tabors never answered.

She heard a movement outside near the bathroom window; she thought she heard a scream?

And then there was a strange whispering on the radio, very quiet at first then as it got louder, she shouted. 'Tabors stop pissing about I need your help, you had better not be fucking pissed again for your sake.'

Tabors never answered, the strange whispering got louder, it was speaking a language Madelyn had never heard before.

She was acquainted with most languages and could speak many, but this dialect was beyond her.

'Who's there, whoever you are I'm going to seriously kick your fucking arse, if you stole that radio, I'm going to make sure you are put away for a fucking long time you thieving bastard.'

Then the voice on the radio started laughing, it was more of a cackle than a laugh.

Madelyn's hairs on her neck and arms stood up, she, all of a sudden was more than a little worried she tried to stand up, but her legs wouldn't move.

Then a pair of grotesque arms came up from the toilet pan and started fondling her, she was frozen to the spot and couldn't even scream.

One of the hands reached up and touched her face the stink was sickening, the arms started fondling her in a suggestive manner she felt a hand go into her pants and remove the flask.

She saw the hands in front of her face, one grabbed her mouth and forced it open the other hand which had the flask was waving it about, she followed the flask desperately wanting a drink.

And then she felt a movement under her in the pan something was pushing her, it pushed her off the pan, she landed face first onto the floor.

She saw stars that gradually disappeared, but the pain didn't. Madelyn struggled to move her eyes, and she somehow managed. And then she saw it... she was so sorry that she had looked, unsure at first whether it was man or beast, then her eyes answered her question, she knew what was coming next.

Her clothes were ripped off her, she prayed hard to die before it happened, but death never came only the searing burning pain came.

She couldn't close her eyes, which may have helped? but it never happened, the pain only got worse. she was just waiting for death to take her, but she never had that option, death was a long way off.

The excruciating pain was her only sensation, then it stopped, the pain eased for a few seconds then returned with a vengeance.

The empty whiskey flask was on the floor close to her face, the spilt contents left a puddle on the floor, she tried to pick it up but was violently thrown across the bathroom; she hit the wall and fell to the floor whimpering, trying desperately to cover her nakedness. She tried to crawl towards the door but was prevented from doing so.

She saw that the being was standing there in all its nakedness, she then knew that it had not finished with her and was ready to take her again and would finish what it had started.

It cackled hideously, and it picked her up and used her as a sex toy, blood was spurting everywhere she swallowed so much of the metallic tasting liquid.

The thing roared loudly and threw her across the room, it started cackling as she watched it disappear down the toilet pan, and she sighed heavily and welcomed the darkness as it wrapped itself around her pain filled body.

Chapter Four.

Hogan was waiting for the doctor to do his rounds. He was ever hopeful that he would be discharged. He'd had more than enough of hospitals, especially this hospital.
When the doctor finally turned up, he examined Jimmy and said he could go home in two days, providing all the tests were good. Hogan shrugged his shoulders and said, 'Two more days won't make a difference I'm good with that.'
He booked a TV for his room and had decided to enjoy the peace and quiet, he was constantly interrupted by nurse's doing tests, but it never really bothered him.
He had a visitor, Mark Laurence, who was the recipient of Geraldine's laptop. He was a very good friend of Hogan; they had shared a few jobs in the past. It was Mark who was responsible for filming the evidence, for quite a few of the investigations, they were a team in the full sense of the word.
'Sorry to see you in hospital mate, I saw exactly how bad it was on the video. I have managed to isolate

certain actions, and shaded in the "things" for want of a better word that you will see if I can show you?' Mark opened the laptop and went through the video. 'This first bit is you in the shower before you get hit, there is a female standing in the shower with you, and it appears that she is naked but as with the other two it is only an outline, that's why I shaded it in.' 'Other two?' 'Don't interrupt just watch and listen. The Female suddenly turns around and starts running, and then disappears through a brick wall. And then, just as suddenly, another thing appears and attacks you.'

You can see when you get hit, and again I have shaded the things? And you can just about make out it's a naked male. He is attacking you, and then another naked male appears and pulls him away and they both start struggling.

Your attacker makes a break and then punches you in the chest, then its goodnight Irene. there must be some sort of naked get-together? It appears, Jimmy boy, that the female has the hots for you and gets caught by her boyfriend?

Then John Wayne comes to the rescue but loses to the bad guy, who carries on where he left off.

I have made a couple of copies of the video in case you ever need it, but there is one thing for sure Jim, and this goes against everything we have ever done together. This is no setup, this is real, and I would go further by saying, and what you are probably already thinking? That they are Ghosts, or spirits of some kind, the real McCoy, Mate.'

Hogan sat looking at the video open-mouthed, not saying a word. He knew that what he just saw, would put him out of work, all his years of disclaiming this sort of thing would come back and kick him in the arse.

'And this is definitely the real thing Mark?'

'I'm afraid it is I have done all the tests possible, and you know if it was a fake, I would find it.'

'Shit Mark you know what that means?'

'I'm afraid I do; it means that we have been wrong... well not so wrong actually because we have never seen anything like this. We have spent years physically searching, and it has proved fruitless, we were "Ghosthunters" Jim, who never actually found anything until now! So, we can turn our careers around and actually show the world what we have found. And the number one disbeliever in the world is getting his arse kicked.'

'The world and his mother would pay good money to see me in that position, but now we have to find out what we are going to do?

But first and foremost, we have to warn Madelyn Clark and tell her what we have found, or better still we have to show her.

I hate the bitch, but we cannot let anything happen to her.'

'Good luck with that she will only accuse you of falsifying it as she does. Anyway, Jim, I'm off, I have a million things to do if you need me you know where I'm at.'

Hogan waved to his friend, but he was already on the phone to Geraldine, it kept going to answer the phone. He left a message telling her to contact him as a matter of urgency.

He laid down and started to drop off, but then he smelt something, it was the most revolting smell he had ever experienced in his life.

He opened his eyes and then saw two drooling dog's face's inches from his.

He tried to sit up, but both the dogs growled, their large teeth were bared, and they looked very sharp, he slowly felt around in the bed and found the panic button.

He kept his finger pressed down tight on it, but no-one came, he lifted his finger and pressed multiple times but still, no-one came.

The obnoxious smell was making him gag.

He looked at the dogs and said 'Lay down' they growled even louder, and their faces came closer.

He could feel their drool dripping onto his face. Then he heard what sounded like fingers clicking.

The dogs slowly backed away keeping Hogan firmly in their sight. 'Lay down my little lovelies' he heard someone say but he could not see anyone, he slowly lifted his head and saw a strange figure sitting in the guest chair looking back at him.

'You can sit up if you wish Mr Hogan, but do it very slowly, my two ladies here are very sensitive and frighten easily, and it's when they are frightened that they turn into flesh-ripping monsters.'

Hogan followed the stranger's advice and slowly sat up keeping his eyes on the stranger and on the two Dogs.

When he sat up, he looked across at the nurses' station, the two nurses looked over at him and wrote something down and then turned away.

He looked at the stranger in his room, He was a scruffy dirty individual, he looked unwashed, he looked as if he had never washed.

There were stains all over his clothes and other bits and pieces of what he thought were bits of leftover food, that fell onto the floor, the smell was so overpowering.

He again looked at the Nurses. 'I'm afraid they can't see me, Jim lad, only you have that power to behold my good looks and charm.'

'Who are you? And what do you want? And what the hell is that smell?'

'And what sort of Smell are you talking about? I can only smell that horrible hospital smell. it's making me gag, but never mind, we all have sacrifices to make, I will put up with it for a little while.'

'But who are you, and what do you want from me, and how the hell did you get in here?'

'Bloody hell you sound like one of my wives; I can't think which one at the moment, but it will come to me.' Hogan was getting red in the face obviously frustrated at this stranger in his room.

'I will say this Slowly, Who the fucking hell are you?' he shouted, the dogs stood up and growled, Hogan's face turned from red to white.

'Ok, Mr Jimmy Hogan, before you have a heart attack and die again, my name is Dankformeister Pilgrabdidler, at your service.

I am a spirit snatcher of repute, and I have been sent here to help you.'
'Help me with what? And what do you mean die again?'
'Die again means exactly that, you die once then die again, did you ever go to school, and learn English?'
'I don't know what you are talking about I never died, first time or second time, you have the wrong man Dank shyster pillbutt, or whatever your name is, now get the fuck out of my room.'
'It's Dankformeister Pilgrabdidler, and if you never died you wouldn't be able to see me, unlike the nurses, so let us try again. Died, you see me, not died you don't see me, what is hard about that and any half brain can see that.'
'So, what exactly do you want?'
'Oh, for Satan's sake, why do I always get the thick bastards? Listen, I have been sent here from hell to help you catch a lost spirit.
It isn't any lost spirit it is the spirit of a multi murdering madman, who was sent to the deepest depths of hell, never to see daylight again.
But unfortunately, he escaped, we don't know how, but we have to catch him before he upsets the status quo between heaven and hell.'
'So, you are telling me that The Devil sent you up here to help me catch an escaped spirit from Hell?'
'By fuck, he's got it, he has only gone, and fucking got it, and here is me thinking he was a thick bastard. Yes, Mr Hogan that is exactly why I am here, well almost. But it is you, who is going to help me, catch that spirit who happens to be the same spirit that

attacked you, and yes you died, more than once, and were resuscitated each time, almost knocking on judgement's door.'

Geraldine opened the door and went to come in. 'Oh, I'm sorry Jimmy I didn't know you had company, I'll come back.'

'Err... No... Geraldine please, can you come right in' shouted Hogan. She came in and acknowledged Hogan's guest, the two dogs came up to her and started licking her playfully. Hogan went to say something, and both dogs growled at him then carried on licking Geraldine's hand. 'Oh, what beautiful dogs these are, but what on earth is that smell?'

'I think it's the dogs.' Said Hogan?

'No, it isn't the dogs they smell ok, she said' they then both looked towards Hogan's guest, who looked away. 'Mr Dingbat or whatever your name is. I thought you said that only people who have died can see you.'

'The name is Dankformeister Pilgrabdidler, and yes that is the truth and Miss Geraldine is one of those, ask her if has she has had a near death experience lately?'

'Yes, that is true but how on earth did you know and who exactly are you, and why do you smell so bad, it's so unhealthy.'

'I'm not going through all that shit again even though you appear to be brighter than your boyfriend.

I will just say it once more I am a spirit snatcher, soul snatcher, or you may know it better as a bounty hunter.
I am searching for the spirit who did you both harm and almost permanently terminated your delicate lives. I need the help of both of you as it happens.'
One of the nurses came in and asked Geraldine and Hogan if they wanted a cup of tea, and then started coughing,
'What on earth is that smell? it is disgusting. I think there must be a drain problem, I will get the caretaker to have a look. I am so sorry we may have to change your room.'
She went out and returned almost immediately with an aerosol air freshener and sprayed the room.
When she had left, Hogan's guest got dirty looks from Geraldine.
'I think you had better go and pay some attention to your personal hygiene Mr dangblaster.'
'I told you it is Mr D… oh just forget it, I will be back with some details to prove that this is seriously life-threatening to you both and people you care about.' The foul-smelling visitor disappeared and took his two dogs with him.
Geraldine looked at Hogan
'I'm afraid someone else has been attacked. Madelyn Clark has been taken to intensive care.
She was almost dead when we found her, she had been unusually quiet so at eight thirty we checked on her, and found her laying on the bathroom floor, naked and blood coming from everywhere.

The police have shut the site down and taken control of everything, they wish to question everyone, as soon as Ms Clarke's injuries have been ascertained.
All she kept shouting was your name, so the police are coming in to question you.
Oh, Jimmy, she was in such a bad state and the smell in the bathroom was worse than that person who just left you...' Before He could respond, she saw her laptop on the side cupboard. 'Have you finished with my laptop?'
'I think you had better take a look and see what is on it, my friend has shaded all the characters in it, and you might be surprised at what he has found.'
Geraldine watched the video, and then her hand covered her mouth as if to cover a scream, she started shaking. Hogan turned off the laptop trying to prevent her from being ill.
'Oh, Jimmy what on earth is going on?'
'Well my friend Mark thinks that a female was watching me in the shower and her boyfriend didn't like it, so he gave me seeing to. And then he was stopped by another spirit but broke away to deliver the mother lode and put me in here.
It is only guesswork on his part, but smelly must have the answers, I only hope he washes before he returns, and could you please explain to me when you had this near-death experience?'
She was just about to explain when there was a knock on the door. They both looked around and saw two men standing there, one was recognisable as Constable John Galloway, but the other was a

stranger. Constable Galloway took it on himself to do the introductions.

'Good afternoon Miss Gilligan, Mr Hogan, this is DCI Grant Goodfellow, he is leading the enquiry into the attack on Ms Clarke.' He then went outside to pick up two chairs for himself and the DCI.

Dci Goodfellow started sniffing; he pulled a face then checked his and Galloway's shoes, in case they had inadvertently trod in something.

'Good Day Mr Hogan, and Miss Gilligan, as I am sure you now know, Ms Madelyn Clarke, the famous television investigator, has been seriously assaulted, and we understand that you, Mr Hogan, and the lady in question have never seen eye to eye, is that correct sir?'

'That is correct detective, and it is well known, through TV and the press, I know you know the reason for it so what is the real reason you are here?'

'Well Sir we would like a sample of DNA to help us with our enquiries, and I would like to know exactly where you were between the hours of six and eight thirty pm last night?'

'Officer, I do not wish to insult your intelligence, but firstly I have been here for a while, all my movements are being tracked by hospital security, in case the person who assaulted me would try to attack me again. And secondly, DNA samples are collected by hospitals as a matter of course, but if you wish to see it done please feel free to get a nurse to collect it.'

'We understand you went walkabout the other day, there was no video of where you went, so how do we know that you never popped out and played fisticuffs with Ms Clarke, and wiped the video? I know you have access to people who can sort out and doctor any problems on your videos to attract more followers.'

'Detective Constable Goodfellow. I cannot seriously believe what I am hearing. I think you are mistaking Mr Hogan with some of the other law-breaking shysters who it appears are above the Law.

I will appoint a lawyer for Mr Hogan, and I will be a witness to your allegations.

His alibi although I see no reason, he needs one can be proved beyond doubt, using the hospital security tape. I have practised Law Constable, and I am advising Mr Hogan to not speak another word until he consults a lawyer. Thank you, now unless you have a warrant, I suggest you leave.'

'My correct title is Detective chief inspector Goodfellow.'

'Well, we will see just how long you retain that title, leave now before I call security.'

The two police officers left, but not before red-faced Constable John Galloway thanked Geraldine and Hogan for their time.

After the police had left Geraldine told Hogan about her experience in the control room, and that she never expected to survive the ordeal. Hogan was seriously worried about her and asked her not to go in there again on her own. I think the smelly dog handler is our only chance to find out what is going on?'.

Dci Goodfellow was angered by Miss Gilligan's, outburst, but decided to wait until he had seen the hospital security video and had the result of Hogan's DNA.

He was confident that Hogan was innocent but had to follow all routes. He didn't get to be Dci by taking short cuts and believing peoples word that they were innocence.

He was just about to leave the hospital when he was called by Dr Battams, who was the doctor in charge of Ms Clarke. He joined Dr Battams, in intensive care. Goodfellow sat down in the rather small cramped office and listened to what Dr Battams had to say.

'Firstly, it is a great surprise to my staff and myself that Ms Clarke is still alive, but I understand she is not one to be easily pushed, and her tenacity is well known. Never the less, officer she is alive, and we are doing our utmost to keep it that way.

She stunk of whiskey; we are awaiting toxicology reports.

She has been violently raped, and all orifices were forcibly penetrated, her sexual organs have been ripped almost beyond repair, and will require endless amounts of surgery.

When we X-rayed, her we found a whiskey bottle embedded deep within her, and I can safely say, because of the severity of the damage, she will never experience childbirth. Equally, her back passage was almost destroyed, and her throat, which required an emergency tracheotomy.

I would hazard a guess officer, even though I know nothing of the law, that it was somebody's intention, to murder her internally, from the inside out. And

furthermore, we believe that either the assailant's sexual organ was much bigger than anything resembling normality, or he had used something equally unnormal.
We have taken swabs and samples and sent them to the police forensic laboratory.
And from there they will contact you.
Ms Clarke is being prepared for her first throat operation, and if all is well tomorrow, we will attempt to rebuild her nether regions, it goes without saying, officer. That this will have a long-lasting effect on the woman's psychiatric condition, that's if she survives all the operations, which will take years to complete.'
He handed Dci Goodfellow a complete report of Ms Clarke's injuries, and the amount of reparation needed, so that she may lead a lifestyle as near normal as possible.
'I know it's a silly question Doctor in view of her injuries, but could you tell me when we will be able to talk to the poor woman, we need to catch this madman before we see a repeat of his work?'
'To be honest officer, we could be talking weeks, if not months, it will be a long slow journey before she is capable of talking, and to prevent any more trauma we will have to place her in an induced Coma until such a time that she has regained sufficient strength of her own.'
'Thank you, doctor, I have to inform you that we will be providing Ms Clarke with 24/7 security, in case her attacker should find out that she is still alive, so I must ask you to keep her condition and her whereabouts private.

If anyone asks about her, could you please contact either me or one of my colleagues.'

Dci Goodfellow had never in all his police experience come across anything as violent as this, he had seen and investigated many rapes and murders, but this was by far the worst, he could never understand how a man could force himself on a woman, let alone causing her injury of any description.

The DCI was an old-fashioned copper and an equally old-fashioned man; he still held doors open for a woman old and young and walked on the outside of the pavement.

He still considered women to be the weaker sex, but in the nicest possible way; he enjoyed being a gentleman, and wasn't overly interested in being politically correct, whether it was right or wrong? He didn't need it, His family instilled in him, manners, and respect for everyone.

His next port of call was the site where the attack had happened; He hoped that there was a video and maybe DNA evidence that would enable him to catch and put away the rapist for a very long time. He had a sneaky suspicious doubt about Hogan and his feud with Madlyn Clarke.

Chapter Five.

Dci Grant Goodfellow and Det Sgt Colin Day arrived at the supposedly haunted house and went straight to the bathroom where the attack on Ms Madlyn Clarke had taken place.
There was congealed blood everywhere, up all the walls and even the ceilings. It looked as though a body had been dragged around the room, up and down the walls.
'But how did the drag marks get on to the ceiling?' was the question Goodfellow asked Sgt Day, and as if that wasn't strange enough, the toilet pan was spotlessly clean?
'It looks as if someone came in and scrubbed the toilet sir, maybe getting rid of any DNA, it looks like a brand-new toilet, but there is no way a normal person could do that on a ceiling with a body of any description.'
'We will have to give that some thought Colin, maybe what we are seeing was staged to confuse us? Have we managed to sort out any video evidence of the actual offence being committed? And is there any news of Tabors Zielinski, Ms Clarke's cameraman?'
'I am afraid Mr Zielenski has just disappeared, Soco has found a number of expensive looking cameras

and video equipment outside on the grass, to the rear of the house. Soco examined them, the memory cards were all blank, they hadn't been used.
The television company have shed loads of video cameras all over the place, so we may see where Mr Zielenski disappeared to?'
Police-constable Jenny Wright interrupted them. 'Excuse me, sir, the technicians are ready to review the TV video system and have asked that you be there, they are waiting for you in the TV control room.'
The two detectives followed Constable Wright to the control room, and she introduced them to two technicians, Andy Grayson, and Paul Minter. Paul acknowledged them and went straight back to pushing and sliding knobs.
'We have found a video which appears to be of a man being attacked if you would like to see for yourselves.' He pressed a button and a rather large screen on the wall powered up.
They watched and clearly saw a man seemingly being attacked but could not see who was attacking him.
'What exactly is going on here, it looks like he is having a fit of some sorts?'
'Ok, sir now I will show you the enhanced version, which is a bit different.'
The two officers watched the video and said nothing, Goodfellow, looked at Andy.
'Could you play that again, because I am not sure what I am seeing'
They watched the video again. 'I can clearly see that the victim is the one and only Jimmy Hogan, and that

is the reason he is in hospital, not as a result of a mugging as we were led to believe, so apart from that are you asking me to believe that his attackers are "Ghosts" is that it?'

'We have checked the video many times and it gives every indication that what you are seeing is indeed Ghosts or unknown spirits of some description. One of the... we will call him a ghost. One of the Ghosts is a rather large individual and well built in the nether regions as you can plainly see in his naked state.'

'To be honest, I do not believe for one minute they are Ghosts, but that big bastard I am sure is the one that raped Ms Clarke, search every video. He is not a ghost; he is a physical being if you need assistance do tell me I will cover it for you.

Once soco has finished I want a complete search of the area including the old house. Colin can you get in touch with Chief superintendent Rankler and tell him.... No, forget that I will tell him.'

Dci Goodfellow called up Supt Rankler and asked for more men to help search for Ms Clarke's attacker, who he knew was hiding in the grounds somewhere.

'I want every available man sir, I think we have disturbed some sort of perverted orgy of some description, the attack on Jimmy Hogan was committed by Two naked men and a naked female. none of which have been located, also Sir I wish to charge Hogan for lying about his attack, and wasting police time...' He was interrupted by a loud scream, he looked around and saw Constable Jenny Wright on the floor, he ran over to pick her up, and then noticed everyone in the room staring speechless at the big TV screen.

He sat Constable Wright on to a chair and got a glass of water he held her head in his arms and fed her the water, her eyes opened, she looked towards the TV and started sobbing.

She was incoherent, he looked towards Sgt Day, who had finally looked away from the screen. 'I'll take her out sir, I think you should see exactly what she saw, I am afraid gruesome is not a strong enough word Sir.'

Sgt Day took Constable Wright outside and sat her down, he called for an ambulance because she was hysterical, he found a female officer and instructed her to go with Wright to the hospital and to keep him informed of her condition, he then left to rejoin Dci Goodfellow.

They had just started playing the video from the beginning, Goodfellow watched closely, wondering what all the excitement was about.

The video started off with a man carrying cameras, he put them down on the grass and started talking through a walkie talkie of some description? He started walking over to what looked like the back of a bathroom, with the pipework that came out of the wall. It was fairly obvious he was shouting at the radio and to whoever was in the bathroom.

Then suddenly he was picked up by something and turned upside down, whoever, or whatever held him up by the ankles. And then they saw the reason Constable Wright screamed.

The man's legs were pulled apart, he was screaming loudly, and struggling, it appeared that his arms were also held by whatever? Then suddenly a large cleaver sliced down and split his body perfectly in two, Blood brains and guts spilt out all over the bathroom wall. The shiny sticky blood glistened in the lights that surrounded the house, then the remains of the body were physically pulled down through the ground and disappeared.

Dci Goodfellow ran out of the control room followed closely by Sgt day, they ran to where the incident happened and stopped just short. There was no sign that anything untoward had happened, no blood splatter anywhere, there were no holes in the ground. No evidence at all to suggest that what they had seen ever happened.

Goodfellow walked back to the control room and asked to see the video again, they had found similar videos of the incident taken at different angles, but they all ended the same way, with the victim disappearing into the ground.

'Colin, I want soco searching every speck of soil from outside that bathroom, but first I want to test the area for blood, what we saw either happened or again it was staged for our benefit? if that is the case I am seriously going to kick arse, regardless of whose arse it is.

If it is real, then the victim is more than likely our missing Mr Zielenski.'

Soco, who were already on the scene brought in extra help, they tested the top of the soil outside the bathroom and they indeed found blood, they took a sample and sent it for tests.

The extra officers requested from Soco arrived and after a short discussion formed a plan on how to approach the site and dig down for more evidence.

They had spent an hour digging when they suddenly stopped!

They had found a shoe, but there was a foot attached to it, and almost opposite there was another shoe again with a foot attached.

The more experienced soco technicians took over. Pictures were being taken all the time, they dug further and found leg bones Fibula and Tibia, that were still attached by sinews, and bits of flesh, most of the flesh had been removed.

One of the technicians was giving a running commentary as each part of the body was uncovered. They slowly dug away the blood-soaked earth and made notes of everything they found.

They soon uncovered the patella, and then the two halves of the pelvic region, again there was the barest of flesh but the skeleton although split in two, each side was held together by sinews.

It took a further two hours before they had reached the skull, which was empty the brain and everything else was gone.

It took another hour before the two halves of the body were laid on a stretcher; bits of torn flesh was visible over most of the skeleton.

All the evidence was recorded, and the skeleton was taken away, to be examined in a more sterile environment.

Dci Goodfellow had seen many murders in his career, but never anything as gruesome as this, he was confident that he was dealing with a sadistic psychopath, maybe more than one?

Soco had handed the site over to him, he organised all his men into two-person search parties and instructed them to look everywhere including under stones or anything that could maybe cover a hidey hole.

And when they had searched everywhere to change over search areas and search again.

He followed the teams and helped them with their search, especially anywhere near the old house, meanwhile. A hired digger was excavating the hole where the skeleton was found, and soon there was a large hole Fifteen-foot-deep and twenty foot wide. He ordered another hole dug, and the excavated soil was dumped into the first hole, but nothing more was found.

The search was going well, every conceivable object was moved, and every little hole in the garden in and around the buildings had been investigated.

The whole property was owned by one man, and that man's wife ended up in the hospital, after supposedly being attacked by a spirit of some sort?

Anyway, Dci Goodfellow had permission from the owner as well as a search warrant to search the inside of the old farmhouse, so every nook and cranny would be searched thoroughly by himself and Sgt Day.

They were just about to move into the house to start the search when a constable approached Goodfellow.

'Sorry to interrupt you, sir, Constable Wright is outside on the road she wishes to see you.'

'Well tell her to come in and talk to me.'

'I'm afraid she refuses to come into the farmyard sir, she has valuable information that you must hear, she will not tell anyone else, and she really is in a bad way, sir.'

'Oh, very well constable but it had better be a bloody good reason.'

Dci Goodfellow begrudgingly walked towards Constable Wright who was sitting in a police patrol car, he tapped the window and she indicated for him to go around the other side of the car.

His face was visibly red, and he was far from amused. She made him get into the car and locked the door after him.

'What on earth is going on Constable? You will have to get used to seeing sights like that on the video and in real life that is why you joined the police. Now, what is it?'

'It wasn't just the video sir it was what was standing beside the TV screen.'

'And what was standing beside the TV constable?'

'Please tell me you saw it, sir, oh please tell me that.'

'I'm afraid I have no idea what you are talking about, I heard you scream and then you were on the floor. Spark out.'

'There was a man, well he looked like a man, but he must have been about eight feet tall sir, he was naked he saw me and smiled and started to come towards me, then I saw that he was aroused sir, and that is all I remember.

But He was real sir I never imagined it, and there is no way I am coming inside again, in fact, sir I am resigning as of this minute.' The woman started crying hysterically, he held her in his arms, and she screamed for him to get away from her. She then started pulling her hair out and screaming in a different language.

He left the car and ordered that she be taken to see a doctor or psychiatrist.

Dci Goodfellow was deep in thought, how did she see something that no-one else saw, or thought she saw, she was a young officer and had not seen anything close to what she saw on the video, but it was strange that she described the man as she did.

He re-joined Sgt Day and told him about Constable Wright's statement about seeing a naked man.

'I am not sure whether she had imagined seeing such a figure of a man, or maybe she really had seen him? But no-one else has seen him? What's your opinion, Colin?'

'I can't rightly say sir, we were all in that room together and we all saw the video of Hogan being attacked, maybe she was just confused?

But just say, for argument's sake that he could make himself visible to, and don't get me wrong on this sir if he could make himself visible to someone who has had an emotional shock? like constable Wright when she saw the video of the guy being sliced up, it affects people differently, as you know.'

'So, are you saying that this naked Chappie is a ghost, Sgt Day?'

'It sounds daft I know sir, but then a ghost, as far as I am aware, would not be able to inflict such physical injuries on our Ms Clarke, and Hogan. And the description Constable Wright gave you matches that same attacker, so he is either a ghost or someone who can pop up through secret passages and doorways? there is no other logical explanation that I can think of.'

'That is why I want every inch of these houses and buildings Checked out.

Someone is trying to make us believe that its ghosts, but I can only believe in what I can see, and what is a fact. We can't prosecute ghosts, Colin, but we can certainly catch the shysters of this world.

They think they are better than everyone else, I want to seriously interview Hogan and his girlfriend because I have a sneaky feeling, they are trying to pull off a sensation of some description, using the TV recording apparatus that they have at their disposal. And, Detective Sgt Day, I am sure it is all to do with how much money they can make. So as soon as he is released from the hospital, I want them both brought to the nick. ok, let's look hard and find some evidence that will put them both in front of a judge.'

Jimmy and Geraldine had tried to visit Ms Clarke, but she was in the operating theatre, there was a police guard outside her room.
They started to head back to Hogan's room when Geraldine started sniffing, and Jimmy joined her, she turned to him and said.

'I think your friend is somewhere near, I can smell his lack of deodorant.' They both looked around them but saw nothing, the smell was, however, getting stronger, as they neared his room, they saw nurses running around with air fresheners.

'I'm afraid that smell has returned Mr Hogan' Nurse James said apologetically.

'We have tried to find out what it is, but we are at a loss. And I'm afraid we have no other rooms available.'

Hogan looked in his room and saw the cause of the smell sitting in the guest chair holding his nose.

'That is ok nurse, I will be going tomorrow so one day will not hurt if you could leave me a couple of those sprays, I would be grateful.' The nurse gave him two canisters of air freshener and then she left, apologising profusely.

Hogan gave one canister to Geraldine and they both proceeded to spray the guest chair, their visitor started coughing and gagging, then suddenly disappeared.

The fumes were getting a little too much for them they also started coughing they opened the windows and breathed in the cool fresh air.

'I wonder if the police have found anything at the house, Geraldine.'

'To be honest Jim, I don't think they know what they are looking for, Clarke's cameraman has disappeared, it might have been him who raped her. there was a strong smell of whiskey when I found her, so maybe they were both drinking in there with the camera's turned off?

I am not allowed on the site until they have done all their investigations, I'm sure we will be seeing that detective again, and maybe get some answers?
We are losing money here by the hour we may have to shut it all down.'
'To be honest, I really don't know what to believe, Geraldine, even though I saw the attack on me, I am just bloody confused, maybe this is all a dream?'
'Oh, it isn't a dream Hogan.' Said a voice from nowhere, they looked around but saw nobody there, then a person they had recognised appeared in the guest chair.
He was different though, he was dressed in an evening suit, he was immaculately dressed, clean shaven, and smelt of aftershave.
'Mr Dankformeister Pilgrabdidler, at your service Madam and Sir'
Geraldine looked him up and down. 'Well Mr P you certainly scrub up well, and where are your dogs may I ask?'
'It's Thursday, they stay home and wash their fur on Thursdays, and I couldn't get them to change their minds, you know what females are like.'
'And to what do we owe the pleasure of this visit Mr Dingbat.'
'There is no need to be personal, Mr Hogan, if you have trouble speaking English then just call me Mr P as did the lovely Miss Gilligan.'
"The Lovely Miss Gilligan?" Ahh is that the reason you have cleaned up Mr D… err Mr P. For "The lovely Miss Gilligan"

'Not in the least Mr Hogan, I have just come from a meeting with the leaders of the highest council, and you two were very much the main subjects of that meeting, along with the escaped prisoners from hell.'
Prisoners! I thought that there was only one escapee?'
'Well not exactly there were quite a few, but we didn't want anyone to know.
We have managed to recapture all of them except for three, two of those are being held prisoner by your attacker. They are trapped, and he is treating them like slaves, but that is neither here nor there, we need your help in capturing the main culprit.'
'And just how do you reckon that is going to happen?'
'Well Mr Hogan, there are two ways that you can help it happen, the first is you have to get Ms Clarke back to the place where she was attacked.'
'That is the most stupidest thing I have ever heard. Firstly, the woman is half dead and undergoing operations, and secondly, she is under police guard. And if I go anywhere near her, I will be arrested. And what the hell would that accomplish anyway.'
'Her attacker has not finished with her, we have to take her back otherwise he will come here and finish the job, and then he will be free to go to the next person, at the moment he has not followed her, but it will happen, and we have very little time.'
'That is a total impossibility, it is just not going to happen, that woman is as I said half dead, there is no way I will endanger her life anymore, you said there are two ways, what is the other way?'

'Well Mr Jimmy Hogan, that depends how brave you are, and I really don't think you have the bottle to undertake such a mission.'
'Mission? What the fuck are you chatting on about?'
'Well I'm afraid it would involve you facing the being that put you here in the first place, that is the mission Mr Hogan, should you wish to accept it?'
'What! How am I supposed to capture a giant that is far bigger and obviously stronger than me and is totally fucking invisible? Haven't you got any superpowers that you use to contain these evil spirits, or will I be the sacrificial lamb?'
'Well, unfortunately, yes, that's exactly what you will be because he hasn't finished with you either Mr Hogan, so you would have to face him.
But we will give you sufficient training and arms to do it, all you have to do is taunt him.
He will try and kill you and take your soul to give him more power, but we will be waiting for him, and will then capture him and send him back to where he belongs.'
'Who is this so-called being? And how come you can't just go and pick him up, because you know where he is? I'm sorry mate but this sounds like a load of old bollocks, it isn't making any sense at all.'
'I'm afraid I cannot give you any details about him, but we have four chances to get him, he will not see us when he is attacking any one of the four people involved.
That is, You, Geraldine, Ms Clarke, and the owner of the house who I believe was also in this hospital but has now left for sunnier climes.

She is still in danger. You have all been attacked and he has the taste of your souls, he will do his utmost to take what he believes belongs to him. And only you can help us.'

'And what if I haven't got the bollocks to face him? What then?'

'Well you can always roll over and play dead, and watch him take the people you know, and it will not be a pretty site.

But that is something you have to ask yourself; will the great Jimmy Hogan stand up and be counted, or is that reserved for your growing army of fans who can only listen to tales to your supposed bravado?'

'You know nothing about me; I stand up for what I believe.'

'But that's just it Jimbo, you believe in nothing but yourself, you are quite happy putting other people down for what they believe in.

You have never had an open mind about anything except your own selfishness. The reason that you have never seen any ghosts, is deep down you don't want to! How could you face your fans if after all this time they found out that you were wrong, and the victims that you publicly put down were right?'

'Once again you are far from the truth, I have stated many times that if I see a Ghost, or spirit, or whatever I will be the first to shout out that I was wrong!'

'But be truthful Hogan, you really never wanted to find anything.'

'I don't know now, to be honest, listening to you, and yes you have a valid argument, but that is all in the past.
I now know I was wrong, and I will address that as soon as I can, so to answer your first question.
I do have the bollocks to see this through. I just do not have the experience or the know-how. And I can't for the life of me understand how you can train me up in such a short time? It sounds like something from a Kung fu film that you see on the telly.'
'Thank you, Jimbo, you have just grown a bit bigger in my eyes, trust me, training you will be easy, in fact, you hardly need any training for what you need to do.
But you do have to pay attention to everything I say, or it could all go wrong in a big way.'
Geraldine had been listening attentively to the two men and her estimate of Jimmy Hogan had indeed gone up in her eyes.
She had grown to like the man but her fondness for him had taken a new path.
'I want to help any way that I can because I feel this is mostly my fault.' She said pleadingly. Jimmy looked at her and shook his head. 'No Geraldine, I can't have it on my conscience if anything happened to you.'
'I wasn't asking you, I was asking Mr P, there must be something that I can do to help?'
'There just might be something you can do, but I will have to take you somewhere else, and explain the plan of attack.

If the plan goes pear-shaped, we may only have one serious attempt at catching him, so we must practise. Where we are going is not the best smelling place you have ever been to, and you will probably recognise the smell.

Right, Mr Hogan, get yourself into bed and just relax, if anyone comes in, they will find you in a deep sleep, Geraldine just leave as normal I will see you both in a few minutes.'

The next thing that Hogan and Geraldine knew they were in what looked like a hotel room looking down at a golden beach with a blue ocean and a blue sky, but then the smell hit them.

It was the same smell as they had first experienced when Mr P first visited them.

The Hotel room was well stocked with refreshments, but the overpowering smell put them both off from trying anything, even the advertised room service did little to tempt them.

'Where are we, Jimmy? I've been to a few exotic places, but I do not recognise this view, maybe its Florida or somewhere like that?'

'I don't even remember lying down in the bed, the next thing I know we are here, but that smell is killing me.'

There was a knock on the door, Mr P walked in before they had a chance to answer.

'Well here we are folks, beautiful scenery, lovely fresh air, what more could you want?'

'Anything but that smell, where the hell are, we.' Geraldine asked holding her nose.

'Oh, please forgive me I have got used to that smell.'
He clicked his fingers and instantly clean fresh air came into the room.
'Where are we, it looks like Florida, or maybe Bermuda, am I close?'
'I'm afraid you couldn't be further away, you are in a place that you have probably heard of, and it's Limbo!'
'No way, Limbo is down in hell somewhere, I'm sure there is no sunshine in Limbo, it supposed to be full of screaming souls, and people waiting to be judged.' Hogan said knowingly.
Mr P walked to the door and held it open. There were ear piercing screams coming from the other side, he closed the door again.
'Oh, quite the expert now are we Mr Hogan? But as you are not in that class it is whatever you want it to be, think happy thoughts while you can.
Right, now, down to business, this is how it's going to go, so I need your One hundred per cent attention.'

Chapter Six.

Dci Goodfellow and Sgt Day had painstakingly searched every inch of the farmyard including both houses, and nothing was found, except a few old bones that had been sent off to the Lab.
Goodfellow was bitterly disappointed that no hiding place was found, He had even got a police helicopter with thermal imaging to search the area again without success.
He went to the control room for a debrief, the mood was gloomy, the teams one by one announced their findings which was nothing. He asked them to make their reports and then go home.
Sgt Day brought over a sandwich and a coffee, for Goodfellow. 'I'm sorry we never found anything sir, and you can't say we didn't try, everyone gave it their all.
I think sir we have to take a step back and have another look and start from scratch if we have to, and as you said, sir, Hogan and miss Gilligan may know more than they are letting on, maybe to protect the television company from their involvement in all of this.'

'I think maybe you are right Colin; he is getting released tomorrow so we will grab both of them and separate them then go in with both barrels.
Anyway, thanks for being so committed Colin, now get your arse home, I'll see you in the office at eight. I want to be at the hospital first thing and be there when Hogan is released, you can be sure that miss Gilligan will be with him.'
Goodfellow had a lot of paperwork to go through, there was now no reason to hang on to the site, there was nothing more to be gained, no clues or evidence was found that would aid the case.
He did, however, get the technical staff to record every new video image that came in. He finished his paperwork then made another coffee.
He sat there writing out a report and in his peripheral vision saw a movement, he turned his head but there was nothing there, his eyes scoured the whole control room but saw nothing.
He went back to the paperwork then heard a cackling, but he could not place where it came from, it stopped, then there was silence. putting it down to tiredness he scooped all the paperwork up and placed it into his briefcase he took a swig of coffee then noticed that one of the videos had switched on and was recording.
He flicked the TV button and it kicked into life straight away.
He noticed that there was a movement in the bathroom where Ms Clarke was raped. 'Got you, you bastard, he picked up his mobile but there was no signal, he picked up a landline phone it was dead.

He looked at the screen again there was a definite movement in the bathroom, someone was in there. 'There must be a secret wall in there somewhere?' he thought to himself. He tried the phones again, both were still dead, he knew what he must do; He had to catch the Rapist and whoever else was in there.

He sent a text on his mobile phone to Sgt Colin Day, even though there was no signal, in the hope that he may get it, and send some back-up?

He left the control room as quietly as possible, it was a bright moonlit night, so the chances were, that he would be seen crossing the yard. He went around the back of the control room, climbed over a fence and onto the main road. He crossed the road and climbed over a small hedge, staying low he crawled about a hundred yards to make sure he wasn't seen.

He then climbed back over the wall and crossed the road, the fence was broken so he squeezed through, he followed the hedge that went close to the new house. He kept tight to the front of the house; the front door was ajar.

As quiet as a mouse he entered the house and made his way towards the bathroom, he stopped suddenly when he heard a sort of growling, but then it was silent.

He waited for a while his heart was beating loud and fast, he could hear it, he started to control his breathing to help him relax, his heart slowed, it was then he realised that he was unarmed, he never even had handcuffs.

He had left everything in his briefcase in his haste to catch the rapist, but he decided to go on, He was decidedly bigger and stronger than Ms Clarke, and he had no qualms about mixing it with someone bigger and uglier than himself.

The house was completely silent, there was no movement at all in the bathroom, he breathed a sigh of relief, the person in the bathroom must have seen him coming and left through some other hidden exit? Certainly, not the front door.

Never the less, he had to make sure, he reached the bathroom and turned on the light, it was just how he had left it earlier, except the blood seemed decidedly thicker and had started to smell.

He remained motionless and listened for any other movement in the house, there was nothing, He looked into the toilet pan then decided he needed to answer the call of nature.

As he was relieving himself, he heard a moan or was it a growl? And thought that he felt a vibration under his feet, but put it down to traffic, and then it was silent again, he went over to the sink and washed his hands.

He looked at his tired face in the mirror, he was looking much older than his years, he saw a movement, then the reflection in the mirror changed, his eyes turned a bright red, his whole face changed, there was some ugly creatures face where his face should be, he tried to move but was stuck firmly to the spot.

He struggled to breathe, all he could hear was a cackling rasping sound, he felt a pressure in his head. He knew then that he was going to die, he had no control over what was happening.

All he could think of was his family at home, his children waiting for him to come through the door so that he could tuck them up into bed and tell them the good versus evil stories that they had always loved. Stories that he made up as he went along, but also stories that came from deep inside his memory.
His front door now seemed a million miles away, he knew that he wouldn't be walking through that door again anytime soon, he cried out.
'leave me alone you bastard, I have a life' Then he screamed out.
The pain was unlike anything he had ever experienced before, his whole body burned, he managed to move his head enough to see what was happening to his body, he regretted looking.
He screamed a blood curdling scream one last time.

Sgt Day had received the text from DCI Goodfellow, he called the station and ordered as many men as possible to get to the site of the TV control room.
He and a van full of uniformed police arrived at the same time he led them to the bathroom as DCI Goodfellow instructed on his text message.
He arrived at the bathroom and gagged when he saw a skeleton on the floor, it was the same condition as the skeleton they had found earlier except this one was in one piece.
There was fresh blood dripping down off the ceiling and the walls, and as before the toilet pan was spotless.

He ordered a search and called soco, and then informed Chief Superintendent Rankler what they had found but could not find Dci Goodfellow.

The site was once again a major crime scene, and as before a search of the whole area was undertaken but nothing was found.

The skeleton was taken away to the forensic laboratory.

Sgt Day had an uneasy feeling that the skeleton belonged to his boss, there were no clothes found. Goodfellows Warrant card and all his other bits were sitting in his briefcase, exactly where he had left them when he started the search earlier in the day.

Chief superintendent Rankler turned up and put Sgt day in charge until a more senior officer could be found but Rankler believed that Goodfellow would turn up.

Sgt day went to the hospital and tried to get to Hogan but was prevented from doing so by the ward sister and was told in no uncertain terms to come back in the morning after the Doctors had done their rounds.

Sgt day went back to the crime scene and ordered another check of the of both houses.

Soco was busy in the bathroom he stood outside the bathroom and stared at the bloody floor. He then asked when they would release the site.

He called superintendent Rankler and asked permission to dig out the bathroom? He never gave a reason, permission was granted.

That would be his first job in the morning after he had spoken to Hogan and his girlfriend. He went home to bed.

Mr P was going through the plan when someone knocked on the door.
He carefully opened the door an inch or two and listened to what his visitor had to say, then closed the door.
He pulled a bottle out of his pocket and took a good swig from it then replaced it in his pocket and looked at Hogan.
'We have a little problem, the target has just got a little stronger, and he has devoured and taken the soul of another Human, someone you may know, Dci Goodfellow.'
'Jesus when… how… what do you mean devoured?' Hogan asked. 'Exactly what it means, he has eaten the detective, the same way he has eaten Tabors Zielinski, Ms Clarke's cameraman.'
'For Fuck's sake, you never said this fucking thing or whatever it is was a cannibal?'
'Just a minor slip up on my part Mr Hogan, it doesn't matter what it is, it has to be stopped before it gets any stronger, now can we get back to discussing the plan, or are you going to chicken out?'
'You knew exactly what it was and what it was capable of doing, and you never told me because you knew that I would never consent to do what we are attempting to do now, preparing me for its dinner.'
'That was a little melodramatic jimmy boy.
We have something that he desperately wants, and that is how we are going to defeat it.'
'Me! It wants to eat me, so are you going to ram a stick up my arse and tempt it into having a kebab?'

'That's a very novel idea, Mr Hogan, maybe we should have that as a plan B, just in case you lose your bottle and drop down dead.'

'Ok, you two that's enough.' Geraldine shouted, 'this is serious enough without you two adding salt to the wound. Now please tell us, Mr P, exactly who we are fighting, and what it is you have, that he wants? And none of your "I can't tell you" bullshit, we are either a team or we are nothing! now sit down and put your cards on the table.'

Mr P looked at Geraldine, and knew that she was serious, he had expected too much from them, yet tried to hide from them the identity of the attacker.

'I am sure you have heard of someone in the distant past called "Vlad the Impaler"?' Hogan and Geraldine both looked at each other and both nodded.

'I'll just give you a few details anyway. Vlad Voivode to give him his official name, Was the fifteenth-century prince of Wallachia, who lived at the time of the Ottoman expansion into Europe.

He was thought to be the cruellest human being ever and had murdered upwards of a hundred thousand people.

These were mostly his enemies, the Ottoman Muslims, but nobody was safe, his many enemies were kept at bay because he impaled thousands of bodies and left them for all to see.

It was rumoured that Sultan Mehmed 11 of the Ottoman empire, fled with his army after seeing twenty thousand impaled corpses rotting on the outskirts of Vlad's capital city Targoviste.

There are many more incidents I can tell you about, and yes, he was also known as Vlad Dracula, son of the devil, which supposedly gave birth to Bram Stokers Dracula.

Anyway, he was getting increasingly more murderous, so the divine powers that be ended his life, and the rumour that he was Immortal.

He died in 1476, and he was sent deep down into the depths of Hades, where it was hoped he would never see the light of day again.

He seemed to accept his fate and assumed that he would be allowed to keep his soul because of his Royalty, of course, there was no chance that could possibly happen.

He threatened to escape and use his dark powers to inflict pain and suffering to the world, on a scale that had never been heard of before.

Of course, he might be in for a surprise when he hears about the two world wars! And various diseases that went on while he was walking around his cell.

Anyway, even though it has taken him over five hundred years to escape, but he has finally done it.

I know that he will be searching for his soul, and that will be his means of capture, but it must be sooner than later before the body toll climbs even higher.

All souls taken from the spirits that have been dispatched to Deep Hades are kept in a secret location, I will go through the plan I have and then I will collect his soul and give to you, and then we can spring the trap.'

'There is just one question that's bugging me! And I really cannot get my head around it no matter how hard I try.' Hogan said.

'Ok' said Mr P. 'hit me, get it out your system.'

'Well we keep hearing about the powers of Heaven and Hell, and they can do this, and that, just by waving their finger, or thought control, so why can't they catch this Vlad guy and put him back where he belongs? Why do they need a Mortal? Like me to try and catch him?'

'Good point Mr Hogan and believe it or not it is all about Politics, the same thing that you have controlling your lives. There are certain things you can and can't do on Earth. And that is the same with Heaven and Earth; it's all about Political Protocol. The People at the top from both Divinities and you know who I mean? Meet up in a great big room somewhere, and Discuss the problems of the day and weigh up the Pros and Cons.

Their first decision is to not get their hands dirty if they can possibly help it. They then pass the "get it sorted" order down the line, and the "Buck" keeps getting lower and lower and stops with people like me.

They are aware at all times of the progress of all such orders and will step in if and when needed, but when they do, they are not best pleased.'

'I can understand that, to a point, but what I meant was what about the Magic, thunderbolts and lightning, the things you read about in the bible, why can't they do that?'

'Again, Mr Hogan It's a bit like royalty, Kings and queens have arse lickers who want to be seen to be doing what they are good at, after they have licked arse, they buck pass, and so on down the line, and unfortunately, I'm at the very end of that line.
Well, I was until you got involved. So, it's all about Political Protocol, and keeping everyone happy, and We know that if they wanted to, they could just wave their arms and wipe every living being off the face of the Earth, and indeed Heaven and Hell, and start again, but they believe in the status Quo, and always hope for the best, without divine intervention.
We lost it now get it back.
And my friend that is where we come in. So now if there are no more questions can we revert to the plan? Time is running away from us'
Hogan stood up and faced Mr P.
'So, who are the other two in the house, a female and another male who had apparently tried to stop the Vlad guy from attacking me without success, who are they? and are they an added danger to our quest?'
'Oh, shit we are never going to get this sorted out in time, the two people or spirits in the house have been taken from limbo by your Mr Vlad, and if it comes to it, they will probably help you in any action against the target.'
'Probably!! Mr P…Probably isn't very reassuring, they could all fancy me as a Kebab for all you know.'
'I give you my word Mr Hogan those two spirits will cause you no harm. Now we really must get back to the plan, if that is alright with both of you?'

Geraldine and Hogan shrugged not really convinced that Mr P was altogether trustworthy.
They both agreed to return to the action plan knowing that it was a deadly serious encounter for Hogan.
It was a long drawn out process of planning that generated more questions than answers.
Geraldine wanted a more hands-on involvement, as a backup, but Hogan and Mr P both disagreed because of the unknown danger, she stood up and looked at both.
'Just bloody listen to yourselves you pair of chauvinists, you are both taking everything for granted, you are just bloody assuming that, that thing is going to roll over and play dead because you have what it wants.
You said yourself, Mr P, that it is getting stronger. So how in the fuck do you know it still wants or needs its soul? It has suddenly started eating people and for what? It surely can't be that fucking hungry, maybe it has outgrown the need for its own soul because it is swallowing new souls? Souls are souls, are they not and I'm sure that detective's soul was a lot more sin-free, as was maybe the cameraman, Tabors Zielinski? It certainly seems to know what it wants, and again you are only assuming you know what it wants?
You have got to provide a backup plan, either to catch it or protect Hogan from it!
 You have to go back to the beginning and work out a different plan of action.

I'm disappointed with you Mr P, you at first appeared to know what you were talking about and pulled us both in, but I can see that you have not even convinced yourself that the plan will work.

You are only going by previous experience where the target was nowhere near as dangerous, now convince me that I am wrong, and I will sit here in my place as a dutiful defenceless female, with my mouth firmly shut! The silence in the room was overpowering. The two men said nothing, they sat staring at Geraldine with their mouths open, and they looked at each other and said nothing, finally after what seemed forever. Mr P spoke.

'If there is something you need to say Miss Gilligan please feel free.' She gave him a stare that would have frozen hell over.

'If you have something to suggest that will aid us please feel free, I am serious Miss Gilligan, I am open-minded enough to hear any ideas.'

'Ok Mr P, here's one, is there not any spell or chant that you can use to send this being back to where he came from as they do in the films? And you have to ask the question they must have got the idea from somewhere?'

'I'm surprised you asked me something like that, Miss Gilligan, it is indeed pure Hollywood glitz, and there are only two people that can do that sort of thing.

And they have passed it down to us to catch him in our own pathetic bumbling way, so they can laugh at us mere mortals or ex mortal in my case.'

'So how did they catch him in the first place?'
'He was dead, weak, still shocked that he was not big enough to stay alive, shocked that he was not immortal. He was easier to control. since then he has got steadily stronger, and yes, you may be right about it swallowing souls. I have not come across that before, so I will have to go and get some information from the powers that be and take their advice.
We will end this meeting, you will wake up at the hospital Hogan, you are to be released today and a certain Detective Sgt wants to talk to you.
I will collect you as soon as I have more answers.'
Hogan opened his eyes, he was in bed in his hospital room, the nurses had come in and opened the curtains.
'My word Mr Hogan you slept well last night, you were snoring slightly and had a smile on your face, were you dreaming about the lovely Miss Gilligan?'
'I think I must have been a nurse, when can I go home?'
'As soon as the Doctor has done his rounds and signs the release forms, there is no set time they get here when they can. There is a detective waiting to speak to you, he came around last night, but the ward sister sent him packing but he has been waiting in the hallway since early this morning, maybe he has found out who attacked you?'

Hogan picked up his towel and toilet bag and went for a shower, he was really tired, he smiled to himself as he remembered Geraldine's outburst not once but twice. He had nothing but admiration for that woman and maybe a bit more, he had an extra long shower and felt so much better, as he turned and went to climb out of the shower enclosure, he saw a man standing there. 'What the fuck do you want? Who are you?'

'I'm detective Sgt Colin Day sir, I wish to ask you a few questions about your supposed mugging, that you reported to Constable Galloway.'

'I never reported anything; you ought to get your facts, straight detective.'

'How come you never mentioned you were attacked in the shower of the supposed haunted house?'

Hogan was not happy at being questioned by this man in these conditions he pulled the panic cord and within seconds nurses came rushing into the shower, they pushed Sgt day out of the bathroom and called security and helped Hogan back to his room.

Sgt day was not amused and decided there and then that he would wait until Hogan was released and take him to the police station to make him sweat. He would find the answers.

But within seconds his phone rang, it was Doctor Battams, the pathologist, he wanted to see him as a matter of urgency.

Sgt day called the police station and ordered an arrest warrant for Hogan and asked for an officer to wait for his release and arrest him.

The pathology dept was an extension to the hospital so he didn't have far to go. Dr Battams was waiting for him and took him into his office.

'I should really offer you a drink Sgt to help steady your nerves, for what I am about to tell you, it isn't going to be easy to and I'm not sure how to start.'

'I'm ex-marines Doctor I've seen many things so give me it straight.'

'Well the two skeletons were in a bad way as you know, and we have spent the night running tests, we are sure that the one from last night was Dci Goodfellow, but we are awaiting DNA results.
The first skeleton is Tabors Zielinski, DNA has confirmed that.
Now we do not know how they died but we can tell you that both bodies had teeth marks all over them. We have taken casts of each bite mark and sent them off, but they looked very similar, meaning one person.
The small amount of flesh that remained had been pulled and chewed as if they were eaten alive.
The skulls were both empty, all that remained was mostly bone and a very small amount of flesh.'

'How could that be doctor, maybe it was some sort of machine that stripped the bodies, probably by the attacker of Ms Clarke.'

'Trust me, officer, if you wish I will take you to the remains and you will see for yourself it was not done by a machine, and it was not an animal.

The teeth marks are human, there is no doubt, and when we get the results from pathology that will back up my claims.

My secretary is just typing up my findings, she will give you a copy, and as soon as I receive the other results, I will send them over to your office.'

Sgt Day left the Pathology dept, not quite believing what he had just heard, it reminded him of a cheap horror film that they made in the sixties.

He made his way back to Hogan's ward in the hope that he was still there.

Constable Galloway who was waiting outside Hogan's ward answered that question. The two policemen paced up and down and drank coffee and then more coffee, they had even read all the magazines in the rack, and they waited patiently for Mr Hogan to be released.

Sgt Day was silently grieving the loss of his friend, Dci Goodfellow, they had been very successful as a partnership and had become very close.

Sgt Day was treated as a member of the Family; he even had a front door key.

He had Gone to the Goodfellow family and shared their tears, they didn't know for sure whether the second skeleton was Goodfellow, but they all had a gut feeling.

Sgt Day tried to keep his feelings professional, but the loss was hard to bear, he didn't mean to come across as a bad copper, but grief is a hard weight to carry alone.

But he would have to deal with it and be strong for The Goodfellow Family when the time came.

Finally, after what seemed to be forever, Jimmy Hogan was released.

Sgt Day approached him again this time there were no nurses to push him away, although they were watching him very closely.

'Good Afternoon Mr Hogan. I am you may recall? Detective Sgt Day and I understand you have met Constable Galloway? We would like you to accompany us to the police station, there are a few questions that I would like to ask you.'

'And if I refuse your invitation Detective, Sgt Day?'

'I'm afraid that will not be a good idea, Mr Hogan, firstly it would give me the impression that you have something to hide, and secondly, I have a warrant here to arrest you if necessary, but I thought that I would offer you the less embarrassing option.'

'Well thank you very much Sgt for your consideration, I shall be delighted to accompany you, please lead on.'

Hogan was led into a rather large interview room at the Police station.

It had a rather large Mirror on one side of the wall, and Hogan knew that there was somebody the other side watching the Interview.

Constable Galloway brought him a cup of tea and a biscuit, "a pretty rare combination" according to constable Galloway.

Hogan sat down and watched Sgt Day flicking through some papers and occasionally glancing up, Hogan had seen it all play out before and knew that Sgt day was biding his time, trying to make him feel nervous.

Sgt Day picked up the papers and squared them all off by banging them on the desk. He then Looked at Hogan and cleared his Throat.

'Mr Hogan, I understand that the reason you were in the hospital, was as a result of a supposed mugging, is that correct? And Constable Galloway was led to believe that was the reason you were incapacitated?' is that true?'

'No, it isn't true, I never gave any inclination as to why I was in the hospital, at that point of the interview I never actually recalled the reason I was there, in Fact, it was Constable Galloway who informed me that I was mugged.'

'But you now know that wasn't the true reason you were there?'

'I have since found out that I was attacked while investigating a supposedly haunted house. I never knew at the time exactly why I was here, But Ms Gilligan has since informed me of what really happened to me.

She was worried that if she told the truth about my attack, I would sue her company which of course I was entitled to do.

Ms Gilligan has not made an official statement and she would like to officially apologise for wasting police time. I can understand how she felt, but once she started the lie it was hard to stop it, so I would also like to apologise for not speaking up.'

'So, Mr Hogan as you were both attempting to pervert the cause of justice, it may have become a habit? What can you truthfully tell me about Ms Clarke and her partner Tabors Zielinski?

I know that you have an alibi being in the hospital, but Miss Gilligan was apparently in very close proximity to where she was attacked, is there anything you wish to tell me that might assist me in this barbaric attack on a woman who you hate and despise.'

Before Hogan could answer another question, Geraldine walked in.

'I'm sure you may know Sgt Day. James Hogan is a client of mine and I wish to consult with him straight away.'

Sgt Day and Constable Galloway stood up straight away and left the room. Then there was silence, Rankler excused himself and five minutes later, Sgt day came in and informed Hogan that he was free to go.

Hogan told Geraldine everything that went on, including allegations that she was a probable suspect, in the attack against Ms Clarke. Geraldine was fuming; she left the room and stormed past Sgt Day, causing him to lose balance. He popped his head into the room and asked if all was well, with miss Gilligan? Hogan laughed, 'I have no Idea Sgt she just stormed out without a word.'

Ten minutes later Geraldine returned with someone in tow, and dragged him into the interview room, she ignored Sgt Day and slammed the door in his face. The Man she had dragged in, she introduced to Hogan, Chief superintendent Rankler.

He sat down and listened as Geraldine bent his ear, she was tapping the table and pointing towards

Hogan, it was all gobbledygook as far as Hogan could make out, all aimed at Sgt Day.

He apologised for His actions, and also to Geraldine, for questions, he had asked about her. They left the Station and went to a restaurant for lunch.
Hogan had never asked what happened at the police station, he waited until she was ready to tell him.
And she did just that, explaining wrongful arrest and various other legal shortcomings that she put to Rankler, who was fully conversant with arrest and questioning protocol.
She stressed however that she felt a little sorry for Sgt Day as he had lost a very close friend and workmate; he was only trying to search for answers.
Rankler called Sgt Day into his office.
'I'm not going to tell you off Sgt, I think I understood where you were coming from, we have all done something similar, and I won't mention it again.
Rankler stood up and went to a little cupboard in his office he
pulled out a bottle and two glasses and poured neat whiskey into them. He offered a Glass to Sgt Day.
'I'm sorry Colin, but I have to inform you that the second remains that were found at the house were the remains of DCI Goodfellow.
I am on my way to officially break the news to the family; I think under the circumstances you should take some time off.'

'With respect sir I do not want time off, and I would like to accompany you when you go to see the Goodfellow Family.
I know them very well sir, and it is my duty to be with them. I apologise for my actions this morning, from this moment on sir, I will be professional in my work.
I know how the DCI would respond and that is how I will respond; it is important to find the person responsible for what they have done.
I would also like to carry on with the dig at the house, I'm sure we will find something there sir.'
'Very well Colin, you can accompany me to see Mrs Goodfellow, and then you can carry on if you feel able.
Mr Mullins, the house owner has given his permission to do whatever is necessary, and in fact, he will be happy when it is demolished. His wife is still suffering from the attack.
She is recovering in the Bahamas, as I'm led to believe so do not worry about damaging the site, the more we can dig out and investigate the better, just give it your best shot Colin.'
'I will sir I will do it for Dci Goodfellow and his family.'

Chapter Seven.

Dankformeister Pilgrabdidler had sought an audience with the powers that be, in regard to finding some sort of assistance enabling the capture of the escaped spirit of Vlad.
They were not the most helpful of powers, but they did offer a little help in the matter.
Mr P was soon joined by Hogan and Geraldine, they were halfway through eating their lunch when they appeared in front of Mr P.
'Thank you for the warning, Mr P, I was just enjoying my lunch.'
'You can eat lunch anytime Mr Hogan, we have a job to do.'
'Did you find any help in capturing this Vlad the Impaler guy, or have we to do it on our own? And while we are on the subject where exactly is, he hiding, is it the new house or the old house?'
'He is in between the two, and down a few hundred feet, he can come and go as he wants, there is a tunnel between the old sewer pipes.'
'Well, that explains the smell that is constantly around us. So, what is our plan of attack Mr P and what assistance can we expect to kick this guys butt?'

'All I have is this Orb.' He held up a multicoloured glass orb so that they could both see it.

'And how does that work? Am I supposed to throw it at him and knock him out long enough so that you can tie him up and send him back to the depths of Hades?'

'Well Mr Hogan that is a lot closer than you think, but all you have to do is touch it with the orb, and it will be returned to Hades.'

'Ok, I'm good with that so all we do is get it up here and let it have it.'

'If only it was that easy Mr Hogan, first you have to find him, and to do that you will have to go to where he is hiding, then you attract his attention and at the correct time you touch him with the orb.'

'And how am I supposed to see him if he is completely invisible?'

'Where you are going, he will not be invisible, you will be able to see him, as clear as day, along with the other two spirits, hopefully, they will help you once they know you have an Orb.'

'And will they be prepared to be returned to wherever it is that they have escaped from?'

'You can leave that part to me and the proper authorities, they are aware of what we are attempting to do and will readily step in and assist us.

Now I have a plan worked out, and it requires both of you to pay attention, you can ask questions as we go, and I will do my best to answer them.'

'Ok Mr P fire away, you have my undivided attention.'

'Right the first stage is I will take you deep down into the depths of the earth.
You will follow different tunnels until you find your target. I will issue you with a map of the area and a suitable torch. But you, of course, have to be prepared because he might find you first, in fact, it would be better if you expected him to find you first.'
'So where do I come in Mr P, I have told you I want to play my part in the capture, I am not going to sit on my backside while Jimmy is facing a great danger. I am not prepared to let him do that on his own.'
'Your part Miss Gilligan will be as equally as dangerous as anything Mr Hogan faces, all will be explained as soon as I have gone through Mr Hogan's part. At the same time, it is important that you know exactly what his role is, so once again please pay attention.'
'I do not want Miss Gilligan to be involved in any danger I have already made that clear, I don't want her anywhere near this evil Bastard.'
'And who gave you permission, Mr James Hogan, to dictate what I can and cannot do? You have absolutely no power over me and cannot control any actions that I decide to take. I respect your concern for my wellbeing, as I do for you.'
'Paleeeeese, you two you sound like an old married couple, if this is handled correctly you will both be safe, so just pay attention to me, we are being watched by the powers upstairs who want it sorted, so listen up.'
'Right the plan is this……'

Detective Sgt Day wasted no time after he and the Supt paid their condolences to the wife and family of Dci Goodfellow.
Sgt day was a close family friend and he promised he would do his utmost to find his friends killer, it was too painful to see his friend's wife suffer in her grief. She had all her family with her sharing that Grief.
Sgt Day made his excuses and left promising that he would visit her soon, hopefully with good news.

He arrived at the haunted house site first thing the next morning, the demolition contractor was already waiting. He would demolish the bathroom and dig up the floor with the assistance of soco, who would be searching the site for any clues to the Killer.
Sgt day informed the machine driver that he was sure that there was an underground entrance somewhere so to dig very carefully.
It appeared that as they dug deeper, the soil that they had dug up was saturated in blood.
 Soco kept taking samples and placed them in a large container, before long they sent that container away and started filling another.
The digging was halted when they discovered human bones, all the bones were collected and bagged, the digging resumed, the depth of the dig was now fifteen foot, and no sign of any underground entrance was found.
 Sgt Day agreed with soco that a further five feet could be excavated, that was the maximum reach of the digging machine.

But before they got that far they started digging into virgin soil, so they were just about to cancel the dig and fill in the hole when the machine driver noticed a hole that appeared just underneath him.
He pointed it out to Sgt day who grabbed a spade and started digging. The hole opened and he saw that there was some sort of broken stone steps.
The machine driver refused to let him anywhere near the hole until it had been inspected and made safe. They called the appropriate people but there would be a long delay.

The owner of the house Mr Richard Mullins and his wife Alice were holidaying in the Bahamas, Alice was recuperating after being attacked at the haunted house, it wasn't the first time, it was a regular occurrence, but she was too scared to tell her husband because it only ever happened when he wasn't there.
The first attack happened when she was in the shower, she felt someone fondling her, she looked around but could see no-one, she found that she couldn't move, at first, she wasn't sure if she had imagined it, but then gradually the attacks got worse and more personal.
The spirit tried to penetrate her many times, but it was too big. But each time it tried harder, and each time she flexed her muscles, something that took a great deal of concentration.
The pain was too much to bear it was pure fear that kept her there, unable to move, each time she was

frozen to the spot, and each time she hoped it would be the last.

Finally, at last, she had got the strength from somewhere she ran out of the bathroom, it picked her up and threw her down the stairs.

Her husband found her and took her to hospital, as he picked her up and lifted her into the car; she looked back and saw the creature, naked and erect. She would never enter that house again.

Richard and Alice were enjoying the wonderful weather of the Bahamas, they had made many friends despite the fact that she had to be pushed around in a wheelchair, but her wounds were almost healed.

They were on their way to the hospital to have the plaster removed from her legs and arms, she was looking forward to wearing her bikini and tanning her lily-white legs, and more than anything else she was looking forward to being intimate with her loving husband Richard, who had remained patient and understanding of her injuries, over the last few weeks.

The nurses at the hospital were kind and gentle, they delicately cut away the plaster, she felt a cool draught when it was removed, and she laughed at the whiteness of her skin.

The nurses massaged her arms and legs and applied moisturiser, she felt like a million dollars, her husband took her shopping and bought her new bikini's and evening dresses so that she could make up for the time she had lost sitting around in itchy plaster.

She was intent on enjoying herself and Promised herself that she would spoil her husband, and thank him for looking after her, and running around fetching and carrying and helping her perform the most basic of hygiene requirements.

After their shopping trip, they returned to their five-star hotel bathed and dressed for an evening of love and promises.

They started the night in a rather expensive restaurant, there was a band and they danced, albeit very carefully, but they danced, tiredness soon caught up with them, so they decided to hit the casino.

They had both been very lucky of late and wanted to keep lady luck rolling.

As the night rolled on her tired arms and legs started to pain her, they decided enough was enough and would finish the evening's entertainment in the privacy of their luxury boudoir.

Richard insisted on bringing her wheelchair at the start of the evening as he knew that she would be tired. So, they took a slow walk back.

Her husband pushed the wheelchair and started singing with apprehension at the promise of the forthcoming attractions.

The Hotel was wheelchair friendly and it was no trouble navigating the different heights of the floors. Lifts were numerous, and sharp-eyed porters picked out the heavy tippers, always a friendly smile in the hope of a backhander containing a few shekels, Euro's or bucks.

Any monetary donation was gratefully received. But that, unfortunately, didn't include the Mullins entourage, because what the Mullins had, the Mullins kept.

The couple reached their luxury suite, Alice stood up from the wheelchair and poured them both a drink, she kissed her husband and stripped off her clothes suggestively and headed towards the bathroom.

Richard followed closely, also stripping off. He was intoxicated by the evening's alcohol and the thought of the sweet nectar that had evaded his attention for so long.

They walked into the large shower and started kissing, touching, and whispering their love for each other. Alice was so excited when she felt her husband trying to enter her from the rear, but then she opened her deliriously lust filled eyes and realised that Richard was in front of her, and both his hands were caressing her ample bosom.

She put a hand behind her and touched something that was not her husband, she forced her husband away then turned around and saw that a shampoo bottle had fallen over and was pointing towards her, she laughed and took hold of her worried husband, she apologised for pushing him, they carried on where they had left off.

Alice took hold of Richard and walked back towards the bedroom, she turned him around and sat him on the bed, he lay down and she crawled onto the bed, kissing him from foot to chin.

He knew that she was ready he guided his body so that he made entry effortless, she sighed as he went deeper into her.

Alice leant forward to kiss her husband then felt a cutting burning sensation enter her from behind, her husband was inside her but someone else had penetrated her. She could not move but could feel as each thrust went deeper inside her, she could feel her flesh tearing on the inside with every thrust and felt her warm blood running down her.

Then the attacker withdrew but as he did, so he took the flesh with him, she fell onto the floor and saw the thing standing there with bits of her flesh dangling from his giant erection.

Richard tried to sit up, but he was frozen to the spot he could not move. He saw the thing looking at him and cackling, then the thing leant over opened its big ugly mouth and bit off Richards blood covered manhood. He took another bite to finish it off then swallowed it all.

Richard tried through the sheer pain to look and see how Alice was, but he couldn't lift his head. he could only hear her screaming, he felt her touch his leg and it sounded as if she called out his name.

The thing whatever it was took a bite out of Richards's abdomen, he saw his entrails hanging out of the creature's mouth like multicoloured spaghetti. the creature stuck his head in his chest cavity and felt the pain in his heart, and then he died.

Alice was screaming in the hope that maybe she had dreamt the whole thing and would soon awake from her nightmare.

But she knew it was no dream and pleaded with her god to end her life. She could not move but knew that she was shaking violently; she was unable to close her eyes she watched as the creature slowly devoured her Husband.

The creature slurped and burped as he gratified himself on the skeletal remains. Then the creature stood up and looked down at Alice and when she saw that he was getting excited she had no more scream left in her, she just wanted death to take her as fast as possible.

But that wasn't going to happen, the thing picked her up and placed her on his engorged member, again she felt her insides being ripped apart. 'Was there no end to the suffering I have to endure before I die.' she asked herself,

When the beast had finished with her, he threw her on the floor like a ragdoll and went back to eating the remains of Richard. It seemed that after a while the beast had stopped moving, it was asleep.

She heard soft snoring, she found that she could move, very slowly but she could move, ever so gently she started to move towards the door, she kept stopping to listen that the thing was still snoring.

It was a long drawn out process, but the door was getting ever nearer, she hoped that she would have the strength to stand up and open the door.

She finally reached the door and took one more look at the thing snoring, she stood up and took the handle of the door and slowly turned it, slowly she pulled the door open, and took a step outside, then suddenly the thing grabbed her and pulled her back into the room.

She screamed as loud as she could, but then her voice failed her, she could scream no more and she could no longer move.
The thing picked Alice up by the head and started cackling loudly. He roughly fondled her body. Every inch of her body was in pain. She saw what was left of her husband and all the blood that they had both lost she knew that death would soon come, but she feared it wouldn't come soon enough.
And she was right, he lifted her up and penetrated her once more, she could feel no more, she looked it in the face and spat into its eyes, the thing cackled louder and reminded her that it was in charge and bought all her pain back. He pounded away with a vengeance and then lifted her off, she thought that was the end but how wrong she was. He forced her mouth open, her last living memories was the gagging, and then her throat being ripped out!

Chapter Eight.

Dankformeister Pilgrabdidler, stood in front of Hogan and Geraldine, holding an orb in each hand.
'Right you two I have explained countless of times to you the plan of attack, so just one more time to be sure.
Hogan, you will be going into the tunnel in the depths of the earth to try and contact Vlad, as soon as you meet him, you have to make sure that he sees the Orb in your hand he will have no special powers down there and will chase you as an ordinary person.
Let him catch you, as soon as he does touch him with the Orb, he will instantly be returned to the deepest depths of hell, and your job will hopefully be done.
If on the other hand you touch him, and he remains there, run like hell to the exit where Geraldine and I will be waiting, we will show him the Orb with his soul, that should slow him sufficiently to allow you to touch him again, and send him on his way, so are there any questions?'
'I still have got serious concerns that this is gonna go shit shaped, and I will be eaten, I haven't got a lot of confidence in your plan Mr P, there is something that is seriously nagging me, but I cannot for the life of me get my head around it.' Hogan said shaking his head.

'Maybe we should all go together to make contact we will know straight away if Mr P's plan works if it doesn't, we Die.'

'Thank you for that thought Geraldine, but there is nothing that can go wrong, the Orb that Hogan has should work straight away, it will definitely work the second time, even though Vlad has gained plenty of strength no one is strong enough to face the Orb twice and survive…' There was a knock at the door, Mr P opened it slightly and listened to the voice on the other side, he thanked him and closed the door, and he looked at Hogan.

'We have just heard that Vlad has killed Mr and Mrs Mullins the owner of the house, they were holidaying in the Bahamas. Vlad obviously wanted what was his, he devoured Mr Mullins and Raped Mrs Mullins to death, there is a slight matter of urgency now, because Mr Hogan you are next on the list, followed by Geraldine, and then Ms Clarke will be finished off, so I suggest we make it sooner than later, like now!'

'I really think we are getting above our punching weight Mr P, he is gaining strength every day, and he really is an unknown quantity.'

'I'm afraid I must agree you with Mr Hogan, but our hands are tied, we have no choice in the matter we have to use the tools we have. But if you want to drop out, I cannot force you, but I will understand.'

'Shit Mr P I am not dropping out I am just looking for another plan B or anything that I can use against it. If I am next in line for the carvery, I want to make sure he gets salmonella or some sort of punishment if he eats me so that I know he won't come after Geraldine.' Again, there was a knock on the door, Mr P carefully opened it a fraction and listened to the person talking, and he took something off him, thanked him and closed the door.

'Well Mr Hogan we have just had a special delivery from the powers that be, they listened to what you just said and gave me this to give to you.'

He passed the object to Hogan.

'It's a glass phial what is it?'

'It is your other plan B Mr Hogan if you fail in your attempt to capture Vlad you are to swallow the contents of that little glass phial as soon as possible, whatever happens, you must swallow every drop.'

'Will this make me live long enough to capture that thing?'

'Err... no… not really Mr Hogan; there is enough poison in there to kill half the population of hell. Extra strength, brewed especially for Vlad, so if you are caught and obviously dying, you drink the poison and it will kill Vlad as soon as he starts nibbling at your vitals.'

'That's it? That's the extra plan B? I am a walking salmonella virus?'

'It was your suggestion Mr Hogan; The powers that be listened to you and are very impressed with your selfless statement and the potential act of Bravery, to save the lives of Geraldine and Ms Clarke. They have at this very moment provisionally reserved a seat for you in the hereafter.'

'Oh… Well… Err if you put it like that then, of course, I will only be too pleased to save the lovely Geraldine from any harm.'

'And do you think the Lovely Geraldine is going to allow you to die such a death, Mr Hogan? I can assure you I will do my damnedest to make sure that no one else Dies. So, do you think we ought to get started on the plan that we already have, and hopefully, there will be no plan B.'

The two men looked at Geraldine, and smiled, they thought it better not to answer her.

Mr P used his magic powers to transport the three of them to the underground tunnel that Vlad was known to travel. He gave the Orb to Hogan and the other one to Geraldine.

She kissed Hogan on the cheek and made her way to the exit where she would be waiting for him, or Vlad, or Both.

Hogan was very nervous, scared really, unsure as to how this would all pan out, His face tingled where Geraldine had kissed him, He regretted not returning the kiss.

His ambition now was to survive if at all possible, and attempt to become friendly with Geraldine, he would go slow with the romance bit because he didn't want to frighten her off.

He knew that there was a very strong bond there, but didn't want to press his luck, he wasn't the easiest person in the world to get on with, but Geraldine seemed to be able to handle him, and that pleased him. She was a strong-willed woman and would make a Beautiful loving wife, whether she would be his wife remained to be seen.

The underground tunnel was dark, he could see in the very far distance the exit where Geraldine and Mr P were waiting for him, and maybe Vlad?

He hoped that he could settle with the big guy in one attempt, he was worried about letting it anywhere near Geraldine.

He paced backwards and forwards always keeping the exit in his vision so that he would know which way to run for his life if need be.

He saw a movement in his peripheral vision and froze, his heart beating overtime, he made sure that he had the Orb in his strongest hand, and then made a silent prayer.

He pushed himself as close as possible to the side of the rough tunnel wall, he shook his head knowing that the creature could probably smell his fear.

He heard shallow raspy breathing and then the smell hit him, it was a very overpowering smell and reminded him of Mr P, the smell got stronger, he could plainly see the monster, now only a couple of yards away.

He waited patiently, his stomach was making all sorts of rumbling sounds, the monster stopped and cocked his ear, it couldn't make out what the rumbling noise was, then it started moving again.

Hogan took that opportunity, and jumped out in front of the monster and hit it in the face with such force that he smashed one of its eyes, there was blood flowing down the monsters face, but it didn't disappear as was expected, all it did was follow the movement of the orb in Hogan's hand. Hogan hit it again, nothing happened, the monster never took his eyes off of the orb,

It was at that point that Hogan realised that Mr P, had given him the wrong orb, he had in his hand the soul of Vlad the Impaler.

Hogan slid down the wall and felt around the floor, he found what he wanted and stood up, the Monster started to make its move and went to grab the orb, Hogan stepped back and produced a rock and went to smash the orb, the monster froze.

Hogan breathed a sigh of relief, he was safe for the moment, happier for knowing that the monster still wanted its soul, but he was unsure of what to do next? If he followed the plan to run to the exit Geraldine would be in danger, and that he didn't want.

Hogan looked around but could no longer see the exit, not that he would have gone to it. He decided to try and follow the trail that the monster had used, although he would be going blindly not knowing where it led to.

He knew which pocket the poison was in, and if the monster was successful in getting the orb, he knew his life would quickly be over.

Slowly Hogan, walked sideways, his back to the wall, not taking his eyes off the monster. He had a good look at the naked monster and although it looked human there were a few differences.

It was a good eight feet tall and probably four feet wide, with huge but natural looking muscles, its skin was a green grey colour, it was sweating, and the smell was nauseating.

When it growled its green brown teeth showed bits of decaying food stuck in between them which had done nothing for its oral hygiene.

But its main feature was its oversized sex organ, it hung down to its ankle's like a spare leg, it was so huge it would have put an elephant to shame, but that wasn't all, there were what looked like outward facing thorns all over the organ.

Hogan understood exactly how much damage could be sustained with such a weapon, he concentrated on the monsters one good eye, and then wondered that if it could suffer that damage, why couldn't it be killed?

The question was answered almost straight away; Hogan looked on in disbelief as the damaged eye repaired itself.

It was now pitch black, the only light source was the orb containing the monster's soul, but because Hogan had a good grip of it, there was limited light showing through.

He kept glancing away looking for an exit of some description, he knew that the monster would make its move before long. He wondered what Geraldine was doing now. Maybe she had gone home thinking that he was dead, and what about Mr P? He must have some sort of inclination that it had all gone shit shaped.

He wondered how he could have lived so long being so stupid. 'Soul Snatcher my arse' he said aloud not caring what the monster thought.

Hogan still searching saw a faint light in the distance, he didn't know how far it was, but it was a chance.
He knew the monster would make its move very soon, Hogan rehearsed in his mind what he would do, and how he would do it, the poison was the only way the monster could be stopped, and Hogan knew he would be eaten the first chance the monster got.
So, it was important that he swallowed the poison as quickly as possible before it went after Geraldine and Ms Clarke.
His plan would be to distract the monster by throwing the orb some distance away, and then take the poison, which of course meant that he would dictate his own demise, not the best of ideas but that was all he could think of, and time was getting on.
The light in the distance was getting nearer, he saw a movement in his peripheral vision, and wondered if it was one of the other two spirits from the haunted house?
He kept going, he decided that he would count down from a thousand and when he reached zero, he would throw the orb and take his life.
Maybe he would return as a ghost and would be able to see Geraldine? He laughed at the thought, all the years he had never believed in ghosts and now he wanted to become one, just to say goodbye to the woman he loved.
He had counted down to two hundred and ninety-one when again he saw a movement in his peripheral vision, he didn't want to turn and look because the creature was watching his every move, ready to pounce at the slightest chance, there was a definite

movement somewhere between him and the exit a little ahead of him.

He stared into the creature's eyes. It gave no indication that it had seen the movement, but it might already know that there is a trap waiting ahead. Still, Hogan defied his overwhelming curiosity to look, he wanted desperately to get the poison from his pocket, but in doing so he would give the creature the vital seconds it needed to snatch the orb out of his hands and put him on the lunchtime menu.

Suddenly the creature turned its head and growled, that was enough time for Hogan to hold the rock and orb in one hand and retrieve the bottle out of his pocket. He popped off the top and put the bottle between his lips, ready for when the creature made his move

But Hogan decided that he wasn't going to wait, he tapped the orb on the creatures face to get his attention away from whatever it was looking at, then he threw the orb and went to drink the poison when he was suddenly grabbed from behind, the sudden attack made him swallow the bottle.

He started choking, whoever held him pulled him clear of the hole and squeezed Hogan's Diaphragm sharply, he coughed up the bottle, it landed on the floor.

Whoever had hold of Hogan released him, he landed on his knees and picked up the bottle, it was only half full.

He swallowed what was left of the poison and stood up, He turned around to see who had grabbed him, and was shocked to see Sgt Day standing there holding up a pair of handcuffs.

Hogan turned towards the hole looking for the creature, but it had gone. He sank to his knees and laughed, then started crying.

He tried to go back through the hole but was grabbed by Sgt Day, who immediately slapped the handcuffs on him.

'You stupid Fucker, let me go, and you should run while you still have the chance, the creature is only after me, the poison I took was not just for me it was to kill the creature, now my life is a waste.'

'I knew you had something to do with this Hogan, and I just saw your friend, in the costume, it never fooled me.

James Hogan, I am arresting you for the murder of Detective Chief Inspector Grant Goodfellow, you do not have to say anything, but it may harm your defence if you do not mention when questioned something which you later rely on in court, anything you do say may be given in evidence, do you understand? Mr Hogan.'

'I understand that I am dying Sgt, and you have fucked up the only chance of destroying that savage creature, now Miss Gilligan and Ms Clarke will die, and you will be responsible.

You should let me go Sgt, or just handcuff me here so that I cannot move, and let the creature take me, I must be sacrificed for the women's sake.'

'Yes, Yes, Yes, Mr Hogan I have got all that. All this was just a publicity stunt so that you and your girlfriend could make money, well Mr Hogan, I believe they still sew mailbags in prison, and you may earn a few bob a week, not exactly Hollywood status, but you will mix with the Infamous murderers and villains, and who knows those mailbags might contain fan mail for you?

Now stand up and let's go I have a car coming to take us to the station, I have another car going to pick up your partner in crime, we will see what sort of bullshit story you both come up with, now move your bloody arse.'

Chapter Nine.

Geraldine was getting impatient she kept going to the entrance trying to gaze through the darkness, looking for Hogan, she thought at one stage that she heard a growl or a muffled scream, but she couldn't make out what it was.
'Something is wrong Mr P, I know it and I can feel it in my chest, I know Jimmy is in Trouble, we must go in there and help him.'
'If we go in there Miss G, we might cock the whole thing up, and put him in even more danger, give it another couple of hours, if nothing happens, I will go in there and have a look around.'
Geraldine paced backwards and forwards sighing at every opportunity so that Mr P would hear her, but he did nothing, he just sat there, silent, not moving a muscle and just stared at the entrance of the tunnel. She was getting very impatient, he looked at her and was about to speak when they both heard a tapping sound coming from very close to the entrance.
Mr P stood up straight away and went towards the entrance, there was another tap, he leant forward and grabbed hold of a rock and pulled open a door that was built into the wall, he opened it just a crack,

and listened to what the person on the other end was saying, he thanked him and closed the door.
Geraldine went over and looked at where the door was, there was nothing there, just rock and grass-covered soil, no opening whatsoever.
'What did I just see Mr P?
Mr P was sitting on his haunches holding his head, she couldn't hear what he was saying, but it certainly didn't sound very encouraging. She shouted.
'Mr P… what the hell is going on and how was there a door there, that isn't there now, and why are you sitting there holding your head, speak to me!'
He looked at her and his face looked very sad she knew then that it was bad news.
'He has got hold of his soul, Miss Geraldine, that murdering monster has got hold of his soul and his strength has now multiplied beyond belief, and it is all my fault.'
'What!! Where is Jimmy, is he alright, will you talk to me…'
'Mr Hogan was arrested by Sgt Day after he took the poison, he was taking him to the police station when he collapsed, he is now in intensive care at the hospital.'
'Ok Mr P go and get an antidote for the poison, straight away before it's too late, I need to go to him. And why is it your fault?'
'I… Err… I gave him the wrong orb, I must have mixed them up somehow, I don't know… I'm so sorry. I'm afraid it is too late miss Geraldine, there is no antidote, it was a one-off designed especially for

that piece of scum, who is now running wild somewhere.

Hogan knew that if he used the poison it was a one-way trip, it just didn't work out because Sgt Day was an unknown quantity. I'm so very sorry.'

'Sorry my arse you pathetic piece of shit, you get me to the hospital now, and then get your sorry arse back to your bosses and demand a cure, he put his life on the line, and you just tell me you are fucking sorry! Well excuse me buster that just isn't good enough, either you get that cure, or you take me to see your boss whoever he is I don't give a toss who they are, but I will kick someone's arse that's for certain now, fucking move!'

In what seemed like milliseconds Geraldine was at the hospital on her own, Sgt Day came up to her and was about to arrest her.

'Just you stay the fuck away from me, this is your entire fault, and we had this under control until you poked your big fucking nose into it.'

'All I know is what I have seen with my own eyes, Miss Gilligan.'

'And what exactly did you see Detective? Tell me. What??'

'I believe that You and Mr Hogan set up these murders to promote your TV station, and it's all about money. My best friend was murdered, and I want answers, I don't care who you are, this time you are under arrest.'

She put both her hands up in the air. 'No Sgt I will come with you as soon as I have seen Hogan, just a couple of minutes, please I will tell you everything, but I have to speak to Hogan.'

'He is in intensive care; on a life support machine most of his organs are not working what was the poison that he took Miss Gilligan?'

'Just let me in there for two minutes Sgt, and I will, I promise to tell you everything.'

The Doctor in charge let her in to see Hogan, he was very pale and gaunt looking, he looked like death itself, she touched his hand the machine beeped, but he remained motionless.

'Please don't die, Jimmy, I love you, please hang on we are trying to get a cure, I know you are a tough bastard stay here don't go anywhere, I need you, Hogan, can you hear me I need you....'

The doctor pulled her away and as the door was closed behind her, she saw a number of strangely dressed people standing around Hogan's bed, she knew that she would never see him again, she cried hysterically, Sgt Day put his arm around her and tried to comfort her.

'Get your hands off me, you're the reason he is in there.' A female constable took over and took her to the police station, they put her in a room and tried to pacify her, and she was inconsolable and kept calling out for Jimmy.

Sgt Day waited for her to calm down and then went in and asked her if she wanted a solicitor, she shook her head, I am qualified to speak for myself, and I want everything recorded, he switched on the recorder and then gave her the Miranda speech, to which she nodded and answered yes.

'I think Miss Geraldine it is time for the truth, we can finish this once and for all, and get on with our lives.'

'You want the Truth? Sgt Day? And when I tell you the truth will you believe it? I think not, you have gone for the easy option, you have from the start believed that Myself and Jimmy Hogan are responsible, you couldn't be further from the truth Sgt. We are the good guys and what I am going to tell you will prove it if only you can believe me.'

'Well Miss Gilligan, the only way to find that out is if you start from the beginning, I have an open mind and I will treat your statement accordingly.'

'Right Sgt, first are you aware that Mr and Mrs Mullins the owners of the house are both dead? They were murdered in the Bahamas.'

'We have only just received that information; how did you know that?'

'Do you believe in Ghosts, spirits, God and the Devil Sgt Day?'

'I have my beliefs Miss Gilligan, and I know that there is something going on in that house but whether it is ghosts or not I remain, shall we say Open minded to such things,'

'And have you ever been close to death Sgt? I mean close enough to see the light at close quarters?'

'I have been there a couple of times Miss Gilligan, but I don't see the relevance of what happened to me, I am more interested in what happened to my friend and the other victims.'

'Can you just bear with me Sgt it has great relevance trust me, one more question and then I am all yours.

Have you ever seen a ghost or something you cannot explain since your brush with death?'

'I'm sorry I am not playing this game anymore you are here to answer questions, now once again, can we start at the beginning?'

'Thank you, Sgt That little outburst gave me the answers that I was looking for, Ok. It all started when we contacted Mr and Mrs Mullins, they said they had a spirit in the house that had assaulted Mrs Mullins and Pushed her down the stairs.

We contacted Jimmy Hogan who is the best in the business, I thought he was an arrogant son of a bitch when I first met him, but the truth is Sgt I had never met a man like Hogan he told it as he saw it, there was no pretence.

He told me about his shall we say disagreement with Ms Clarke, she really was an obnoxious person, but when Hogan found out that she was in more danger he was the first to stand up and be counted. Anyway, I am getting in front of myself. Now, this is the unbelievable part, so clear your mind Sgt.

We had a visitor in the hospital who wasn't shall we say a normal person, He said that he was a "Soul Searcher" or Bounty Hunter, now if you saw this person you would laugh because he looks nothing like a bounty hunter, and to be honest he never done a lot to prove his worth but you only had to look at him to...' she stopped and saw that Sgt Day had turned a deathly white colour.

'Is this person Miss Gilligan, A small scruffy man with two Doberman Pinschers by any chance?'

'Oh Sgt Day, yes does that mean you have seen this man somewhere?'

'Err… yes, Miss Gilligan; he is standing right behind you.'

She stood up and turned around the dogs came straight to her and started licking her hands. She looked up at Mr P. 'I really hope you are standing there with good news Mr P or I will forget that I am a lady.'

'And I brought the dogs along for protection! Huh, bleeding Girl Power.'

Sgt Day stood up and the dogs growled ferociously, he sat down again.

'Do you possibly think that I could get some sort of explanation from somebody? Or should I just sit here and mind my own business?'

'I am sorry Sgt Day, please let me introduce you to Mr Dankformeister Pilgrabdidler, hells soul catcher extraordinaire or supposed to be.'

'Pleased to meet you Mr Err… Danker pill err…?'

'Just call him Mr P, but quickly I am looking for answers.'

'Well excuse me, Miss Gilligan, I am trying to run a murder investigation here, so who is going to start telling me what is going on?'

Geraldine took the onus and told everything that had happened from day one up until the present time, he sat there open-mouthed.

'And now Sgt if you will excuse me, I need answers myself from Mr P here, and if I don't get them someone is going to get seriously hurt, so what have you got for me Mr P and believe me it had better be good we are running out of time.

Hogan is very weak as we speak, did you get what I asked for?'

Before Mr P could answer there was a knock on the door, a young constable walked in and gave a note to Sgt Day, then without looking at anyone walked out, and the room was silent. Sgt Day stood up and looked at Geraldine.

'I am so very sorry Miss Gilligan, James Hogan passed away a few minutes ago, they tried to revive him, but everything just stopped working.'

Geraldine could not hold back the emotion, she cried unashamedly, then turned to Mr P.

'Get out of my sight you useless piece of worthless shit. It is your entire fault, why couldn't you get hold of someone else to kill?' Mr Ps two dogs whined as if they knew that she had suffered a loss. They stood up and joined their master as he disappeared back to wherever it was that he had come from.

Chapter Ten.

Geraldine left the police station and went home alone; she had refused any help. Sgt Day was very understanding and asked if when she was strong enough, would she come down and help him go through some paperwork?

He wanted to end any association of the murders to her and Hogan.

Sgt Day sat at his desk and tried to understand and get his head around the whole situation.

There was apparently a spirit that had escaped from hell running around eating people, but how could he report that? they would send him straight to the funny farm and throw away the key, He had no idea how to progress with the case, no-one to look for, no-one to arrest, absolute jack shit.

'I wonder how the fuck you would sort this one out grant. I'm sure you would know.'

'Well, why not ask me, Colin, I'm only this far away from my desk.'

Sgt day jumped out of his chair and fell on to the floor, he looked up and Dci Grant Goodfellow was sitting in his chair, looking at the paperwork lying on the desk.

'Sorry Colin didn't mean to make you jump I have been waiting for the invitation to try and help you out, you were a bit slow.'

'I… is that really you sir?'

'Yes, Colin it is me in the flesh… I'm sorry I didn't mean to say that under the circumstances, thank you for looking after my wife, she has taken it really bad and she is not strong enough at the moment to see me.

I must say I was totally wrong about Mr Hogan and Miss Gilligan, everything that they told you was the truth.

I have been thinking about this and the only way I can think of sorting it out is to say that the murderer is now in the Bahamas.

They are always trying to save money, so they might believe that. I will advise you as and when, but from this side, we have the problem of trying to catch that beast somehow, you saw it and thought that it was someone in fancy dress, but I must tell you, Colin, He is one mean ugly fucker.'

'How the hell are you going to catch him, sir, apparently, he has more powers now that he has his own soul back, and he is still eating souls, and according to what Miss Gilligan said she is next on the list followed by Ms Clark?'

'I don't know how we are going to do it Colin, but we have to try, or there will be a bloody massacre, all down to Mr Vlad the Impaler.'

'Who is we, sir? You keep saying we. How many of you are there? And are you all…'

'Ghosts Colin, that's what we are now, not exactly how I thought I would end up, well not this young anyway, the word "WE" includes our friend Jimmy Hogan, and a Mr Dankformeister Pilgrabdidler, whom I assume you have met?
Apparently, Mr Hogan and I had special dispensation to become "Ghosts" because of the nature of our deaths. Mr and Mrs Mullins, and Tabors Zielinski, I'm afraid never got that privileged offer, they were sent to Limbo, apparently, they were not the most honest of people, but that's neither here nor there.
First and foremost, I have to try and protect Miss Gilligan and although Ms Clarke, has not been the most respectable of people, I promised to try and help save everyone I could.'
'Ok sir, so what happens afterwards? Once the baddy has been put away, what happens to you then? Do you go to heaven or hell?'
'Well as far as I can make out, there is no hurry to send us anywhere, it was pointed out that if we successfully conclude the business in hand there would be… shall we say future employment for all three of us? But I'm not at liberty to discuss anything at the moment, Colin.
But you will be the first to know when that happens, meanwhile, we have a serious job to do, now, while I'm here I will make myself useful and help you sort out some of that paperwork, but at the moment I can't quite touch things so if you lay the paperwork out I can help sort it out, just like old times ay Colin?'

Geraldine was sitting in her bedroom watching the video of Hogan in the Shower Room. She froze the screen and touched it tenderly.

'I loved you, Jimmy, I wish I told you how I felt about you, I might have been able to persuade you not to go, not to put your life on the line to try and catch that thing.

It was all that bastard Mr Ps fault. Oh, Jimmy, I would give anything to see you one more time, to hear your voice, to see you smile when I tell you that I love you. Just one more time is all I ask.'

The Laptop fizzled into life she dropped it on the floor, when she picked it up there was a picture of Hogan, on the screen, he was looking back and smiling at her. 'I love you too Geraldine.'

She dropped the laptop again and stood up shaking, she stared at the laptop her eyes filled with tears, Oh Jimmy how… when did you put that on there?'

She laughed and bent down to pick up the laptop, she heard Hogan's voice coming from the laptop.

'I didn't wish to scare you, Geraldine, please don't be afraid, I am a little different from the last time you saw me, please… I err… I don't want to scare you, but I am in the room with you, if you want to see me just turn around slowly, it may be too much to comprehend and may be too much of a shock. But if it is, sit down and close your eyes and I will disappear again until you are ready.'

She quickly turned around and dropped the laptop again when she saw Hogan standing there, one of her hands covered her mouth, and the other stretched out towards Him.

'Oh my God Jimmy… it… it is you, you look different, so… different, can I touch you, Jimmy? Can I hold you in my arms and say what I should have said before you… before you so bravely gave your life'?
'There is nothing I want more Geraldine than to hold you close to me, I will try my hardest to make it happen, I regret not returning your kiss when I left you.
I regret not telling you that I loved you, I regret so much not being able to hold you in my arms.'
'Oh, Jimmy I hope this is not a dream because I have missed you so much, just looking at you now means so much to me.
I love you too Jimmy and I am sorry I never shared those feelings with you. Can you stay with me so that we can catch up to the time that was taken from us my Darling?'
'As much as I would love to spend time in your presence Geraldine, this was only a fleeting visit, I have to meet up with the others and somehow formulate a plan to send that evil piece of shit back to where it belongs. And I am looking forward to kicking his arse all the way there.'
'Who are the others Jimmy, I hope it doesn't involve that bungling idiot, Mr P, it is his fault that you were killed.'

'It wasn't really his fault alone Geraldine, there were a number of reasons, why it happened, all of them unforeseen.
I cannot believe it happened, but I bear no grudge, my only sadness is having to wait to touch and hold you. Mr P is a good man Geraldine and Detective Goodfellow is here to help us, there are three of us and we are no longer weak mortals, we will have the extra power to catch this monster.'
'So, what is the plan of attack, how can I help Jimmy? What can I do?'
'I have no idea at the moment what is going to happen, but I will return and let you know, our ultimate aim is to protect you and Ms Clarke, and anyone else who is threatened by the monster and his friends.
I must go now my sweet, I look forward to our time together.'
Hogan said goodbye and then disappeared Geraldine collapsed onto her knees and cried, she felt that she would never see Hogan again, and thought maybe that she had imagined him being there.
She felt an incredible emptiness and loneliness, in her heart, feelings that she had only known when she had lost her Mother years ago.
She screamed out to her god to send him back to her, he had made the supreme sacrifice in trying to save others he was worthy of being returned.
She picked up the laptop that now had a cracked screen, straight across the only picture that she had of Jimmy Hogan. She held it close to her bosom.

Mr P and Dci Goodfellow were patiently waiting for Hogan when he turned up, they saw the heaviness in his heart, his face was sad and noticeable were the tears that flowed freely down his face.

He sat down and looked apologetically at the recently deceased police officer.

'If it's of any Consolation Detective Goodfellow, I know how you feel, I would like to offer my condolences to you and your Family.'

'Thank you, Mr Hogan, please call me Grant, I would like to offer the same, and apologise for thinking that you were in any way involved in the attack on Ms Clarke, I just put two and two together as usual, and got it wrong.'

'No problem Grant, just call me Hogan and what happened between us in the past has long gone.' He offered his hand and Grant accepted.

'Ok you two I know things are going to seem very strange to you, but I have been there, although it was a long time ago, and I can answer any questions that you may have, but I will say whatever it is that you want to do it takes practice, very hard practice.

I need you to be able to carry certain things so start learning to pick things up, remember this it is more mental than physical, once you have the basics of those two factors they will come together as one.

Mr P pushed the two newcomers as hard as he could, it was at first comical to watch as they tried to pick up little scraps of paper, but then they became very competitive, he used that to his advantage and pushed them even harder.

He knew that they could take it, they had both been strong determined people in their previous life.
Those two attributes would serve them well in their new life, and they would get stronger in time as each new task presented itself.

Mr P. had to physically stop the men from doing any more, they were becoming tired and were making silly mistakes both trying to outdo each other and getting more frustrated.

'Right that's it take a breather, switch off and relax, I'm glad to see that you don't give in easily.

But I need you to stop and rest, empty your minds and when you have sufficiently rested, we will sit down and discuss how we are going to attack the problem in hand, you have got the basics of being able to touch and lift things, and to be honest, it will become easier to you as we progress in finding this creature.'

Hogan stood up and addressed Mr P. 'There is something that is bugging both myself and Grant, and that is, why are there not any ghosts flying around, we thought that as we were now "Dead" we would see them all over the place, so could you be clear that up for us?'

'That is an easy one Hogan, firstly you were visited by Ghosts when you were recovering in Hospital, and they really were your family, your Parents, Grandparent's aunties and uncles, but at the time you were confused and sent them away, you will see them again when you are mind ready, call them they will appear. As far as I am aware you have had visitors Grant, but you have not been as receptive as

Hogan, the same advice I gave to Hogan, applies to you too.

Now secondly! This is something that may come as a surprise to both of you, Ghosts are very shy, very private individuals, and contrary to popular belief they are nothing like anything you have been led to believe in, or otherwise as in Hogan's case.

I'll try and explain, Ghosts are sometimes but not very often "Seen", that is maybe because they weren't ready to go to the higher level, because of missing their loved ones, it takes time for them to accept that they have passed on and try to return home.

Now, some other Ghosts that are seen, have been dragged away from their natural progression, by so-called spiritualists, who have for whatever reason called these spirits and subjected them to ridiculous tests and questions.

The spirit is easily confused and loses track of where it actually supposed to be in the natural progression of the hereafter.

So, it is trapped inside a secondary Limbo, and only an experienced professional Exorcist can send it safely back on its original journey.

So, Mr Hogan, ghosts do exist, and when you were so insistent that they were figments of people's imagination and completely non-existent, what you were doing, and you were very good at it, by the way. Was to leave the ghosts in peace, if you can understand that?'

'Yes, I think that all makes sense now that I have heard it like that. I'm glad that I was doing some good, even though I wasn't aware of it.'

'Will there ever be a time when I will be able to touch my Wife and my Children? By touching, I mean holding like we used to do.

Although I never held them as much as I should have, I would give anything to hold them now and tell them how much I love and miss them.'

'If it is any consolation Grant, I know how you feel, I left my family in the long and distant past.

I feel as you do, and I wish I could tell you it gets easier, but my friend it really doesn't, I have to be truthful. I'm afraid if there was any way that I could help you I surely would.'

Hogan put his arm around Grant. 'We will make this creature pay for what it has done, I miss my Geraldine, but you have suffered far more, we have a job in front of us and we must prevent that "thing" from creating more heartbreak.'

Mr P was happy as he saw the two men Bond and he knew that their determination to defeat the creature was boundless. He gave them a few minutes.

'Right gentlemen, we have things to discuss, the orb that was supposed to send the creature back to hell was mixed up by me, and that is the reason that Hogan lost his life. I accept that it was my fault and that I totally mishandled the situation, and for that, all I can do is apologise.

I went back to the powers that be and they were not too pleased that through my cock-up I allowed another life to be taken. Even so, I asked for their help, they were talking about taking me off the case and replacing me.

But I reminded them that this was the only time I had slipped up in centuries of being a spirit snatcher, Soul Catcher, or a bounty hunter. They in their superior wisdom allowed me to carry on, and what's more, I now have extra orbs, to cover all eventualities.

Now as far as the plan goes I have only one, but I think you will disagree Hogan, but I really can't see that we have a choice.'

'So why don't you say what it is then I can make up my mind.'

'Well, it involves Geraldine, and Ms Clarke, as you know they are both next in line to be revisited by Vlad, we have to be prepared for it, and be in the right place waiting for it to happen then we can pounce.'

'Correct me if I'm wrong Mr P, but are you suggesting we use these women as bait? After what happened to me you can bet your boots I will disagree.'

'I know, and I can understand Mr Hogan, maybe you have a better plan, because I have searched all avenues, and found no other way to catch this creature. I have even asked the powers that be, and without them actually getting involved, which they refuse, there is no other way.'

'I have not even thought about it, to be honest. Maybe deep down I am scared, Mr P. I don't really know, but I will do everything to keep Geraldine safe, and of course Ms Clarke, I do not want them to end up the way we are.'

'Then we must protect them! And the only way we can protect them, Mr Hogan, is by putting them directly in the line of fire, all three of us will be there to protect them, and we will be in the right place at the right time.

I know it is hard for you to believe in me, but please trust me on this one, if we don't act then they will be surely lost.'

The three sat in the room speechless and looking at each other in turn. And as much as none of them wanted to go ahead and put the women in danger. It was inevitable that Hogan and Grant finally understood there was no other way and agreed to listen to Mr Ps plan.'

'Ok, firstly we have to make sure that Geraldine and Ms Clarke, are willing to put themselves in this position, and if they are, we may need Sgt Day to assist us in putting everything together.

The two women must be together in the same room. And then it will be up to us to catch the creature before he can touch either woman.' Grant stood up. 'I know that you can count on Sgt Day to help, although the poor man is totally confused over everything that has gone on.

I will go and talk to him and explain our plan. we have no choice of where we can do this, as Ms Clarke is still in intensive care, so it will be a private room in the hospital.'

'I will go and ask Geraldine. It frightens me to know that she will be only too glad to do her part, but I really am scared for her safety.'

'Please trust me, Mr Hogan, I have the greatest respect for Miss Geraldine, and I would protect her with my life if I still had one. But I fear we can waste no more time in this matter, we must set this up straight away.'

Grant and Hogan disappeared and went to seek assistance from Sgt Day, And Geraldine, knowing what their answer would be, they then would meet up as soon as Sgt Day had set it up.

Ms Clarke was still in an induced coma; Sgt Day obtained permission to have her moved to a private room for protection purposes, he would stay with her until everyone was in position.

He was unsure of what exactly he would do while all the action was going on. He desperately wanted to be part of it, but there was little he could do. Grant had told him precisely what was going to happen.

Sgt Day wasn't a religious man but couldn't help praying to… well, he didn't really have a god as such but hoped that any God would listen to his prayer so that no one else could be brutally murdered by that thing!

Chapter Eleven.

Sgt day had organised the moving of Ms Clarke and sat with her, the doctors had decided to bring her out of the Coma to do tests on her, she was very weak. But he asked them not to put her back into a coma. gradually she came around and saw Sgt day sitting there looking at her, she tried to sit up but was unable to do so.

'Who are you, and where the hell am I?'

'I'm detective Sgt Colin Day, Ms Clarke, you are in hospital, and I have been assigned to keep an eye on you, is there anything you need, shall I get a doctor?'

'Do I look that bad to you? And am I under some sort of arrest Sgt Day?'

'No, you are not under arrest Ms Clarke, you were attacked, and I am here in case your attacker should return.'

'Attack me? Who would attack me? Unless it was Tabors, he gets a bit violent now and…… Oh my God, it wasn't Tabors, it was… I don't know… It was a mons…'

She never finished she just screamed out and started shaking violently, two nurses came running in and tried to pacify her, she started throwing herself around, one of the nurses gave her an injection, and she slowly relaxed then closed her eyes and succumbed to the darkness.

'What was that injection nurse? She didn't want to go back into a coma.'

'It was just something to relax her she will soon open her eyes again.'

Sgt Day was joined by Geraldine, he told her about Ms Clarke.'

'I think she remembered the attack Miss Gilligan, and she was frightened. That is what I think set her off, she will wake up soon and I think she will hurt herself when she remembers again what happened.'

'Call me Geraldine, Colin isn't it?' 'Yes, Miss... err Geraldine.'

'Ok Colin, when Ms Clarke wakes up, I will be here, and I will try to talk to her and pacify her, and hopefully try to explain what is going to happen, without frightening her.

She is a hard woman to talk to at the best of times, but fingers crossed I will be lucky.'

Hogan was alone with Mr P, Grant had gone to see his family, he had decided that he wouldn't try to contact her until after they had finished this Job, but just wanted to see his wife and kids.

'Mr P, I would like to ask you for two favours, one is very important, and the other... well, that is equally important, one I think you would be able to do, and the other one involves putting in a request to the powers that be on my behalf.'

'Well I can't promise anything Hogan but tell me I will see what I can do?'

Grant went to his house and watched his family sitting silently at the dinner table, this was not their usual behaviour.

His wife and two children were playing with their food, not eating it, His wife Angela excused herself and ran upstairs.

She ran into their bedroom and threw herself onto the bed and cried into a pillow so as not to upset the children downstairs.

Grant sat on the edge of the bed and went to put his hand on her shoulder but stopped himself. He felt the pain that she was feeling, he felt her loss, and he felt useless knowing that he was so near yet so far away.

There was a knock on the bedroom, and door before she could answer the two children came in and joined her on the bed, the three cried in unison.

Grant felt that his heart would soon explode with grief. He could not hold back the tears; the grief caught up with him, he screamed out. 'Noooooooo.'

His wife and children sat up and looked around, they had heard him cry out, he felt even worse and decided to leave them lest he break their hearts even more.

Grant joined Hogan and Mr P, they said nothing, and they felt his grief and knew that he was suffering.

'Right Grant, Hogan, the sooner we get this sorted the sooner we will be able to move on and find something else to do.'

He went through the plan again and handed out the orbs. Then went straight to the hospital where they joined up with Geraldine, and Sgt Day.

Geraldine was so happy to be reunited with Hogan, clumsily they touched but it required a lot more practise before that would happen. He took her to one side and spoke to her.

'I need you to do me a favour Geraldine, I need you to get a message to Ms Clarke and give her something which may help her, I know that she is in a bad way, but I am hoping that this may aid her recovery, and I need you to tell her that I am sorry that she is where she is.'

The couple kissed amateurishly but made that vital contact, their hearts beat a little faster.

Mr P stood in the middle of the room and spoke to everyone.

'Right we all know what is going to happen, and we all know what we have to do. I'm sorry I don't know how long we will have to wait here but I'm thinking it won't be that long.

Sgt Day, you are aware that you have to wait outside and keep everyone out of here if, at all possible, I'm sure you can think of something logical to make sure we are not disturbed, and that will be straight away if you please Sgt.'

Sgt Day had done as requested and left the room, thinking up excuses why no-one would be allowed in. The team took up their places, Ms Clarke was coming around and recognised Geraldine she smiled, Geraldine spoke to her quietly and passed on Hogan's message.

'Are the Camera's rolling Sweetie, I hope you catch my good side wherever that is now, I don't suppose there is a great deal to choose from? I was a bitch in

my life, Geraldine, everyone knew it but nobody except Hogan ever had the guts to say anything.
You might like him, my dear, but unfortunately the man has no money and no prospects, but he has his word and that is all he needs.
Up until now my dear I thought I hated him, but he is one of a kind, if he was corruptible, he could have been a millionaire, all he had to do was lie and turn a blind eye. But not Mr Hogan.
Anyway, my dear Geraldine, could you please have a peak and see how bad my once beautiful body is, I can move my hands but nothing else is obeying me.'
'I'm Sorry Ms Clarke you have bandages everywhere it would take me too long to unwrap everything, and there is a chance that I may infect you in some way when I can look, I will tell you.'
'Bless you, child, for listening to me, I remember most of what was done to me, I suppose that I am lucky that I am still breathing but thank you.'
Ms Clarke started to ramble on and eventually fell asleep; Geraldine turned off the lights and waited for the nightmare to begin.
All that could be heard in the darkened room was the gentle breathing of Ms Clarke and the occasional beep of the machine that was attached to her. Nobody spoke, each other aware that silence was important. Mr P, Hogan, and Grant would be invisible to the creature; it would only see Geraldine and Ms Clarke, unprotected and ripe for the taking.
Geraldine was tired but too frightened to close her eyes, but she felt a little safer knowing that she was guarded by Hogan, who she hoped was close by.

The silence was interrupted by one of the nurses who was arguing with Sgt day, she pushed past him and entered the room and switched on the lights, she almost jumped out of her skin when she saw Geraldine in the guest chair near the Bed.

'Who are you? And what are you doing here; you are not supposed to be here.' Sgt Day entered the room a little embarrassed, and dishevelled.

'We are police officers on protection duty we were told no one would be entering this room tonight, so why are you here nurse?'

'I have no such information constable, it is my job to check blood pressure and temperature and that is what I will do, and if you try to stop me, I will defend myself, with my Karate skills.'

'My rank is sergeant Nurse, I will not touch you, and I will leave you to do your job.'

'Thank you, Sgt Day.'

The nurse completed the tests and made notes and checked the bandages on Ms Clarke when she was satisfied that all was well, she turned the lights off and left the room.

She winked at Sgt day and wiggled her butt, and turned to see if he was looking, he was.

'I'll be back in two hours Sergeant; in case you miss me?' He smiled and sat down slightly amused at her demeanour.

Geraldine sat listening to Ms Clarke's steady almost hypnotic breathing and she felt her eyes getting heavy, her own breathing slowed as she started to drop off. Then she suddenly opened her eyes as she felt the temperature in the room drop sharply, she

stood up and looked closely at Ms Clarke's face, who whispered.
'It's here Geraldine, it's come to finish me off please do something.' Geraldine could see nothing but could smell the stink that started to fill the room, she squinted her eyes and searched the room but still could see nothing.
Ms Clarke's heart started to beat faster, and her face turned deathly pale.
'It's tearing at the bandages Geraldine please don't let it touch me again.' Geraldine pulled the covers off the bed and saw the bandages hanging there but could see nothing moving, then she made out a very faint face next to Ms Clarke's face. She picked up a container of talcum powder and shook it over the bed, the creature was revealed, it was naked and trying to penetrate Ms Clarke's body.
It growled at her and she was unable to move, she froze, she tried to call out Hogan's name but was unable to move.
Suddenly the creature let out a blood-curdling scream, Geraldine was free to move, and pushed an orb into the creature's mouth as far as she possibly could, the creature tried to close its mouth, but was unable to do so.
The orb was now pushed down through its throat, she pulled her arm out of its mouth and stuffed a roll of bandages into its gaping hole, that's when she noticed all the blood which covered Ms Clarke's Body.
And then Hogan, Grant, and Mr P appeared, Hogan and Grant stuffed their orbs in the creature's mouth,

Mr P rammed his orb into the only other place available, the creature unable to scream wriggled around and managed to fall off of the bed, it struggled to stand up clutching its throat, it was then that Geraldine noticed that the creature was missing a vital piece of its anatomy.

It tried to remain standing but was becoming weaker, bits of its body were turning to dust, it was dying. Mr P pushed his hand deep into the creature's chest and pulled out the orb containing its soul, the creature turned to dust and vanished, there was silence. Hogan stared in disbelief at the ease in which the creature was dispatched, and then he laughed as he saw Ms Clarke weakly waving something around in her blood covered Hands. At the same, time, he winced.

'I got the bastard right where it hurt, it will never be able to hurt anyone again. That's what happens when you cross me' She burst into tears, and sobbed loudly, Geraldine tried to console her. But had thought that it was perhaps better that she let out all her anger and frustration, she done just that and fell asleep with a smile on her face, and not letting go of her prized possession.

Sgt Day walked in and almost had a heart attack when he saw all the blood, he laughed when he found out that it was the creature's blood, then without warning the nurse returned and stood there screaming.

Mr P touched her on the shoulder, she smiled at him and started to Clean Ms Clarke and reapply her bandages, when she had finished Mr P again touched

her and Sgt Day walked her out and they started chatting, phone numbers were exchanged, it seemed that romance can bloom anywhere, anytime.
Geraldine was very tired but happy that no one was hurt, Hogan walked her home and stood outside till she was safely indoors, he was just about to walk away when she called and ran out to him.
She held him long enough to kiss him before her arms went through his body, she walked back to her house and closed the door behind her.
Hogan sadly walked away.
Mr P called a debrief meeting. Himself, Grant and Hogan were sitting talking about how easy the capture of the creature went.
'I can tell you that I was expecting more of a fight from the creature, it was a bit of an anti-climax, but at the same time, I am more than happy that no one got hurt. But I can't really understand how Ms Clarke was able to cut the creatures john Thomas off as easily as she did, her being so weak as it were?' Grant said shaking his head in bewilderment.
'That had a lot to do with Hogan, Grant.
He suggested going to the powers that be and getting a knife that had been blessed and would be an extra back up for Ms Clarke in case anything went pear-shaped.
But I too am glad to say I am happy that no one was hurt, but I wasn't expecting her to do the damage that she did, but it certainly made our job easier.
I can tell you that the creature is no more, it doesn't exist, it has been vaporised and the only two things that remain is its true history, and of course, the

souvenir which Ms Clarke has decided to keep, well she earned it.

I understand that Sgt Colin Day with Grant's help has cleared up the official Police inquiry, although it is still an open case, it has been sent down to the vaults.

The Police in the Bahamas are still looking for Mr and Mrs Mullins murderer, so it will stay over there. Right Gentlemen, we have had a couple of urgent jobs that have just been passed down to me.

It appears that we will be away for quite a while, many months maybe longer. So, if you want to see your loved ones and whisper sweet nothings or whatever it is that you do.'

Grant stood up almost immediately, 'How long do I have to see my Family Mr P?'

'Hmm, what time do you have Hogan? My watch needs a deep clean.'

'It's ten past ten, and this is a top of the range atomic watch, always right.'

'Well, in that case, Grant you will have fifty, will that be enough time?'

'Fifty minutes? I will make it enough time thank you Mr P.'

'I didn't mean minutes grant; I meant a slightly longer time than that.'

'Would it be fifty hours? That would be more than enough time.'

'I'm sorry for playing with you Grant, I mean you have exactly fifty years to do whatever it is you need to do, and then maybe we will see you again with a happy face?'

'I'm sorry Mr P you have completely lost me, what is happening?'
'It appears Grant that your services are no longer required, you are to be reunited with your family. And everything will be as it was before you met your demise at the creature's hands.
We have adjusted all the paperwork and wiped out memories, so when you go home it will be as it was, and you will carry on with the last job that you were involved in.'
'But how can that be? My body is no more, it was destroyed. How can I look at my family if they will not recognise me?'
'Ok, now all this is Hogan's idea, he begged me to go upstairs and speak for you and plead your case so that you can be where you are most needed.
And that is with your family, and they have given you exactly fifty years to enjoy your life, go and join your Family.'
Grant stood there not quite believing what he had just heard, he had a confused look on his face, Hogan stood up and took a hold of his hand and shook it vigorously.
'Goodbye Grant it was a pleasure getting to know you, the next time we meet you will not remember me, I wish you and your Family well.'
'Thank you, Hogan, and thank you, Mr P., it has certainly been an experience, and one I would like to remember, but I know that will not be practical. Maybe we will still be friends in fifty years time? Thank you.'

Hogan walked him to the door and watched as Grant followed the short hallway towards another door, he went through that door towards the rest of his life, and Hogan was more than happy that was happening.

'Ok Mr P what are these other jobs we have? And are they urgent?'

At the moment Hogan, there are no other jobs, it might be advisable to spend a bit of time with Geraldine while you can.

I am going to fill in that tunnel that the creature used because I am not sure how far it actually goes, but it will keep me busy.'

'Thank you Mr P I will take you up on that offer, I certainly need to practise being able to hold her in my arms for a while.'

'There is I'm afraid bad news as far as that is concerned Hogan, the powers that be have told me in no uncertain terms that you and Geraldine are to part company, you have until I return to try and get that message across to her.

You will never be able to stay together as normal. I'm sorry Hogan it is completely out of my hands.'

'But that is not fair, she played her part in the capture of that creature, and I think she should be rewarded in some way?'

'Well… err… She has been rewarded Hogan, her life was meant to be taken that night in the hospital, but because she helped to kill the creature she was spared.

And if she wasn't spared you would still have been apart, so all you are doing is prolonging the inevitable.

When I return, they will wipe her memory of everything that happened since before the creature first attacked you, I'm afraid that you die in her arms before she fell in love with you.

Please forgive me, Hogan, I went down on my knees and begged that you and Grant should be returned to your proper lives, but they would only give Grant his life because you selflessly asked me to ask for that favour. I am so very sorry, my friend.

I will take my time while I am away, but they will be watching me and will not be fooled if there was any other way Hogan, I… I… Forgive me.'

Mr P disappeared, Hogan sat down on the chair, he could not believe what he had just heard since he had died, he hoped that there was some way that He and Geraldine could be together, he wasn't supposed to die, but he did all because of a cock up.

He searched his brain for a way to try and tell Geraldine the truth, but there was no easy way, in fact, he knew that there was no way!

He knew that there would be no way that he could hold her and kiss her, to him it would feel immoral knowing what the final outcome would be.

He decided to chase after Mr P to arrange to wipe her memory now so that he would not have to lie to her and treat her falsely.

He could never be that person, He loved and respected her too much, but he was Dead, she was very much alive what's not to understand?'

Chapter Twelve.

Mr P had just entered the tunnel when he heard Hogan calling out his name. He stopped and waited till Hogan had caught up to him when he did, he was breathless and had to sit down till he had caught his breath.

'Mr P, I have been thinking and have decided that there is no other way that I can see Geraldine anymore, it would mean lying to her and even using her, and I can't do that to her. So, I want you to arrange her memory wipe straight away please if you can do that for me now, I will be grateful.'

'You never cease to amaze me, Hogan, that is some sacrifice you have just made, but I need you to be absolutely sure that is what you want. I am so sorry that you find yourself in this position after all that you have done, but it is out of my hands.'

'Just do it Please, do it now, I am sure she is waiting for me, do it. Tell me how to fill in this tunnel and I will start while you are away.'

'All you have to do Hogan is dig a hole in the roof every few yards, the weight will force it to collapse, just listen out for the rumble and stay clear.
I will only be gone a few minutes, stay safe my friend.'

Mr P disappeared. Hogan followed the seemingly never-ending tunnel, his mind filled with nothing else but memories of Geraldine. Maybe it would help if his own memory was wiped, but no that was being selfish to himself. it would be a pleasure to constantly see her in his mind whenever he wanted, but he would always make sure that he stayed away from her.

He carried on through the darkened trail chasing his memories, then suddenly he heard voices and growling of some description.

He stopped and listened, there was silence the only sound he could hear was his breathing. Then the strange voices started talking again, he strained his eyes and saw what looked like an opening in the wall directly in front of him.

Slowly he followed the sound, the wall went around a corner, he saw a light appear, silently he peaked around the corner and was sorry that he did so, for directly in front of him were two creatures identical to the creature that they had destroyed so easily in the hospital.

Hogan's Brain froze for a few seconds, he had a dilemma? Should he dig the roof and collapse the trail, or should he return and hope to find Mr P for advice?

He chose the latter because if they were buried, they could pop up anywhere, this way they would know exactly where they were.

He slowly and quietly retraced his steps, and when he was far enough away, he ran as fast as he could and kept running until he ran into Mr P.

'What's the hurry, Hogan, you surely couldn't have done that much damage already, I have only been away a short time.'
'Don't stop, we need to find somewhere safe straight away.'
Mr P grabbed hold of Hogan and before he knew it, he was safely back in the schoolroom that they had used to plan the attack on the Creature.
'What on earth is wrong Hogan, you had me worried.'
'I reached the end of the Trail, and heard voices and growling, I slowly followed the sounds around a corner and then I saw Two creatures the same as the one we destroyed. So, what is that all about? There is no saying exactly how many there are so what the hell are they, they can't all be Vlads, and why hasn't "The Powers that be" mentioned them?'
'Are you really sure that is what you saw Hogan, maybe you are still upset and imagined them, to try to ease your conscience?'
'I cannot believe you just said that you should know me better than that… Wait a minute why do I suddenly get the feeling that you are not that surprised? I feel that there is more. Hang on have I been set up for this again?
You knew that I couldn't lie to Geraldine and that I would come running after you. And you purposely sent me up that trail, knowing I would come across those creatures. You Bastard, I could have walked straight into a trap, was that the plan all along? Have you played me for an Idiot?'

'No Hogan it wasn't a setup, least not by me, I just found out when I asked them to wipe Geraldine's memory, they told me that they wanted to protect Grant and Geraldine, and everyone who was connected to the original creature from this new threat.
And thought it better that we were no longer connected to them, there are two of them and this is their hideout. We must rearm ourselves and work out how to trap and destroy them before they attack any civilians, I am as innocent as you Hogan, believe me.'
'But you lied to me when I ran into you, and you asked me what was wrong? And then told me that I imagined it, so I think there is a bit of a trust issue rearing its head?'
'No Hogan you are wrong, I just hoped that you hadn't seen anything until I told you about them.
I just thought you set the roof to fall. And you were running to safety, well shall we say that's what I was hoping?'
'Ok just humour me. Just say for argument's sake, I never saw those creatures and just inadvertently carried on trying to collapse the roof, what would have been your next step? would it have been along the lines of?
"Oh, by the way, Hogan I have just heard that there are two creatures trapped in the tunnel?"
It really isn't making much sense to me, so tell me exactly what this is all about, leave nothing out, except the Bullshit, I am fast losing my patience, and my trust in you, so this had better be good.'

'Ok, you remember the other two spirits who you saw in the video of your attack in the shower?'

'I'm hardly likely to forget that am I?'

'No, sorry...Well anyway, those two spirits were held against their will by... We will still refer to him as Vlad, so we don't get confused.

Now, these two spirits originally were the good guys, and they promised their help in catching Vlad. So, when we had finally defeated the creature, I went looking for those two spirits, but could not find them. It was a job I temporarily put off, and to be honest with you Hogan, I kind of forgot about them, it was only when I went upstairs to the powers that be that I found out that they were, in fact, hiding in the tunnel. And that... err... they had now become creature's exactly the same as Vlad, and we believe he turned them that way by taking their blood as in Vampires? They have as yet not taken any lives, but I have been told that it is only a matter of time before things change, so we must catch them and send them to the appropriate place before its too late.'

'I don't think that I am going to like what is coming my way, Mr P?'

'They are at the moment nowhere near as strong as Vlad, but that will change the moment they take a life and a soul, then we are in serious trouble.'

'These spirits, can they attack me and... well, I know that I am dead but is there anything more that they can do to me?'

'Not at the moment, but them swallowing souls will not be good for you.'

'Ok so what sort of plan do you have, and I hope this time that you can get it right, we need to do something straight away, so let's talk.'

'I have some new orbs, these are the real McCoy, all we have to do is go into the tunnel and get them to attack us then we will send them home.'

'I feel a little Déjà Vu here Mr P, the last time didn't work out too well.'

'This time you really can trust me, all we have to do is somehow block off the other end of the tunnel where they are, and force them to come to us, what could be more easier than that.'

'And exactly how are we going to do that, or do I want to know?'

'I'm afraid Hogan we have very little choice, you will return to where you saw them and throw a small explosive device, then run back before it explodes. I will be waiting there for you and together we will catch them.'

'I almost knew it would be something like that, show me what armaments you have, I hope this is going to work for my sake, Can I die twice?'

'You really don't want to know the answer to that one. And I am not going to tell you.' Mr P said with his fingers crossed.

The two men formulated the plan of attack, no time was wasted they went straight to the tunnel, it seemed darker than last time. But they couldn't take a torch in case the creatures saw it.

They slowly, and silently felt their way along the tunnel listening for any sounds that the creatures may make.

Hogan recognised the bend in the tunnel and stopped Mr P from going any further.

Hogan took the device and made sure that Mr P had the orbs ready at hand. Hogan crept towards the area where he had last seen the creatures; he carefully poked his head around the corner and had a bit of a shock.

Standing there absolutely Naked, was a young couple, both normal looking human beings, he gasped, they both turned around and screamed then turned into the ugly creatures that he first saw.

He tried to throw the explosive but they both rushed past him and sent him flying.

Hogan screamed out.

'Look out Mr P they are coming your way, get ready.'

Hogan picked himself up and ran back out into the tunnel, there was a loud scream and he heard dogs barking.

He reached Mr P and found him on his knees covered in blood, and two dogs snarling and ready to pounce at Hogan. He recognised the dogs as the ones that he first saw at the hospital. 'Mr P… Mr P…, did you get them?'

'I got one of them Hogan, the male, it is now on its way to hell's fire and damnation, the other one was too fast?'

'They were both normal, but then they turned into those ugly stinking creatures, was that normal?? I didn't imagine that; the woman was beautiful.'

'Their change was not fully complete that is why they walked straight into me; they were ill prepared.'

'So where is all the blood coming from, are you hurt? Let me see.'
'No Hogan I'm good, I took a leaf out of Ms Clarke's book and used a knife just in case, I sliced its manhood off, that one of the dogs caught in its mouth, that was the scream you heard.
But again, it was very easy. But what I'm worried about is where would the other one go to?
I'm hoping that it isn't looking for something to eat or maybe soul searching? We have to find it before it knows we are looking for it?'
Meanwhile, we can blow the tunnel and make our way to the haunted house, I am sure that is where the creature will be.'
They blew a whole section of tunnel in one explosive attempt, they made holes every couple of yards and slowly the tunnel collapsed.
Exhausted they both sat down and rested, their bones weary from the constant digging, even the dogs were weary.
Mr P gave them water from a flask that he carried, they gulped the water, then laid down and fell asleep.
'Is this shit gonna start all over again Mr P? Are Geraldine and Ms Clarke back in danger, have we gone full circle and it's all been a waste?'
'I don't believe they are in danger Hogan, this creature has, as far as I know, had no physical connection to either of them, but we cannot become complacent and we can't stop until we have destroyed it.'

'Could this creature be saved? Is there any way it can revert back to what it was before it was changed by that Vlad creature?'

'Only by divine intervention Hogan, and I can't see them getting off their arses to help this unfortunate "Thing" otherwise they would have suggested it when they told me about them.'

'Well why don't you go and ask them, or better still take me there and I will ask, we have a chance to help this poor soul, who has been put into this situation through no fault of her own.

And they are supposed to reward the good, and the victims of evil although they haven't done too much of that lately, so I think you ought to introduce me to the powers that be, so I can put forward her case, and end any more bloodshed.'

'I'm afraid you have no chance of standing in front of them pleading anyone's case, it doesn't work like that, there is a certain protocol that has to be followed and in thousands of years this has never been breached.'

'So why don't you do something good for a change and carry that young woman's soul upstairs and ask for clemency, let them be seen rewarding the innocent, prevent evil before it happens, what have they got to lose?'

'Ok Hogan, I will take your plea upstairs and see what they say but to be honest, I already know the answer, but I will go regardless.'

Mr P disappeared, and Hogan carried on digging holes in the ceiling, his mind raced back to Geraldine, and his heart missed a beat.

He wondered what she was doing, whether she had completely forgotten about him, he wanted to look at her just one more time but knew the pain would be hard to bear, he dug harder into the roof, suddenly he was aware of a movement to the side of him.

He turned around to face the movement and was shocked at what he saw. It was the naked woman who had run away from him earlier, she was trying to cover her modesty and crying, she looked him in the face and sobbed.

Why did you kill my Husband, he saved your life, your friend mutilated him and sent him away, why? We never did you any harm, we tried to help you and warn you when you were in the shower, but you could not hear us because you are a non believer in anything except yourself.

We were prisoners of that evil creature.

He threatened each of us with the other one's death, even so, we were still ready to help you. Now all you want is to hurt us both, why?'

Hogan removed his jacket and gave it to the female, she hesitated at first but then accepted it.

'I am sorry, but we were as frightened as you when you turned into those creatures, we thought that you were the same as Vlad and intended to kill us.'

'You were wrong we have fought hard not to change into those creatures, but you frightened us, and in that split second we became weak and changed.

We would have done you no harm because we were getting stronger now that evil creature was dead, soon the creature would disappear from us.

Now I am on my own, what should I do Mr Hogan, how do you think I should spend my time? The whole eternity alone, even if I return to hell, I will be alone. We were sentenced to spend the eternity together because we took our own lives after losing someone and not being able to handle the grief, that was our only crime Mr Hogan I…'

She stopped speaking and threw her hands up and covered her mouth, looking at something behind him, he turned around and saw Mr P with a young man standing beside him.

Hogan recognised the young man from the tunnel, he had changed into a creature, and was despatched by Mr P so why was he standing there?

The young man pushed past Hogan and ran to his wife they held each other tight and both shed tears of joy and whispered to each other, they turned towards Hogan, and the young man spoke.

'We both thank you, Mr Hogan, for selflessly saving our lives we have been given another chance thanks to you, and your goodness, thank you, we both hope that your life is rewarded, we will think of you forever.'

The couple waved, there was a sudden whoosh and they both disappeared.

'What on earth did you do Mr P? And what is the story with those two?'

'Well it is a bit sad really, I have only just found out, they were a young couple who met and fell in love, they both worked hard and saved enough to buy a little home.

She became pregnant and they were both very happy at that news because they were both orphans and had been brought up in different homes.
They had been passed from pillar to post. But they met when they were both sixteen, and instantly fell in love. They had a beautiful daughter and there was no one happier.
Their lives revolved around the child, but when she was two years old, the doctors found a tumour on the brain, it was incurable, the child died, and the couple were inconsolable, they had no counselling to help them with their grieving.
They could not handle it and took their own lives, their punishment was light owing to the sadness of the case, but at least they would be together forever.
Even though it was hell, they were reasonably happy despite their everlasting grieving until Vlad kidnapped them.
The rest is as they say History.
They will now be returned and reunited with their child, and they will all live happily ever after.'
'So, you went up there and argued the case for one of them and ended up helping a whole Family, thank you, Mr P, you are the Man.'
'It was nothing to do with Me Hogan, they heard you upstairs and because of that, I'm afraid that we have to part company.
It was their decision, you rubbed them up the wrong way, and they were not best pleased, to say the least. It was thunderbolts and lightning up there, I haven't seen the like for years.

I have enjoyed your company, Hogan, and I will miss you, there aren't many like you around here, in fact, there isn't anyone like you here.'

'I'm good with that Mr P. I am ready for any punishment they wish to hand out, at least I can take that memory with me.

And I will be forever grateful that I saw that young couple being spared and given the chance they deserve.

And even Grant got reunited with his Family, so yes Mr P send or take me to wherever? I am ready.'

'I'm afraid it isn't going to be that easy, Hogan, we have a lot of work to do first I want this tunnel filled in as soon as possible.

And then we have to sit down and work out how the hell I'm going to send you back to Miss Gilligan, without her losing her marbles?

We have to reinstate her memory and put you in the most logical place to make that memory fall into place.'

'Wha... wha... what are you saying, Mr P? Are you saying that I can return to my life and the love of my life, is that what you are saying?'

'Why do I keep getting the thick ones? Yes, Hogan that is exactly what I am saying, you have friends upstairs. Even though they think you are a cheeky bastard, and the fellow downstairs put in a good word for you.

They have decided to reunite you to the life you left behind, and Its true mate, I will miss you, you have learnt something on this strange journey Hogan.

I hope you can take that with you and look at life differently, with an open mind.
And you know what I am talking about, anyway, we have work to do, and not only that I will have to find a new assistant I keep losing them.'
'To be honest Mr P I think goodness bounces off of you, you try to hide so much. I apologise for constantly having a go at you, it's been an experience and I won't forget you that's for sure. And I think that maybe anyone who has met you will never forget you, Geraldine, especially.
'I also have to remind you, Hogan, that it's a bit like being in the Army, you have done your time, but there is always a little bit more needed from you. You are officially in reserve in case I can't find another idiot to help.'
'Feel free Mr P but don't forget, where I go Geraldine will want to go.

Chapter Thirteen.

Geraldine was pleased that the creature had finally been dispatched to wherever, she was waiting to catch a glimpse of Hogan, but thought that he was maybe avoiding her, they had much to talk about.
Ms Clarke was a great deal happier and would not let her prized possession out of her sight until she had made a few phone calls and a messenger came to pick it up, she watched closely as he put it into a secure box along with instructions, she then rested always with a smile on her face.
Sgt Day called in to see Geraldine and informed her that the case was officially closed, and thanked her for helping with their enquiries, she was about to say goodbye when DCI Grant Goodfellow came into the hospital waiting room.
He too thanked her and apologised unreservedly for thinking that she and Hogan were involved in any way in the investigation.
She stared pale-faced and open-mouthed at the DCI.
'Is there anything wrong Miss Gilligan you look as if you have seen a...' 'Ghost' she finished his sentence.
'Are you alright Miss Gilligan should I call a doctor? You don't look at all well Sgt Day asked her.

Dci Goodfellow grabbed the attention of a passing nurse. Geraldine looked again at the DCI and then fainted.

'Geraldine it's me Hogan, are you alright my Darling?'

Geraldine opened her eyes and saw Hogan holding her hand and waving a bit of paper, fanning her; she looked at him and smiled, and held his hand.

'Hogan I can touch you, but I'm confused, am I dead? Grant is here as well I must have died fighting that evil creature, did it kill us all?'

'Everything is ok Geraldine, No one is dead. We are all safe, did you bang your head or something my sweet, and shall I ask the Doctor to look at you?'

He winked at her and smiled.

'It's all over Geraldine the police have closed the case, and everything will get back to normal, and I mean everything Geraldine.'

She looked at Hogan and rubbed the skin on his hand then reached up and touched his lips.

'Such manly lips Hogan. I want to taste them now.'

At that everyone excused themselves and left the room, they were alone.

'Kiss me, Hogan, you have never kissed me properly, and it's about time that you did, and then I think you owe me an explanation.'

Hogan explained the whole story, leaving out nothing. She cried with happiness at the thought of the young couple being reunited, and Dci Goodfellow going home to his family.

But more than that she cried tears of joy for her own happiness, she would be with the only man that she had ever loved.

Hogan Married Geraldine and they went on to produce their own investigative television show which aired all over the world.

The programme was called Geraldine's Ghost's and the chief ghost finder was James Hogan, assisted by the one and only Ms Clarke, who walked with a permanent limp but was aided by a special original, one-off walking stick, that was insured for millions.

It was obvious to everyone who saw it exactly what it was, and it had been tested but all the scientists declared it was from some visiting alien.

She had been offered multi-millions for the stick but would not let it go, money meant nothing to her anymore, because she had her memories.

And now she had friends, something that she never had before, her friends, who would stand by her through thick and thin, they were the family that she never had, the family that she would never lose.

She was Godmother to Hogan and Geraldine's eldest daughter, and she would give her life to protect her if necessary and give her the love and guidance that she herself never had.

But had learned everything from the Friendship of Geraldine, And her very good friend Hogan.

Mr P would show his face every now and again and made his feelings for Ms Clarke known, she was interested in him but was unsure of his intentions and wanted to know more about him.

He was a changed man and was always impeccably dressed. Thanks to Geraldine for giving him those well-needed fashion tips.
His dogs were also part of the ever-growing Hogan family, and they would readily stand guard when Business called them away,
And the business did call them away, regularly.
Mr P and Hogan had a special friendship and they would look at each problem and work out the best way to address it, and always without fail, they would have a plan B... Just in case.

The end

Authored by

James P Gavin

Printed in Poland
by Amazon Fulfillment
Poland Sp. z o.o., Wrocław